THE GAUNTLET

IMDALIND ACADEMY, BOOK ONE

REBECCA ETHINGTON

IMDALIND PRESS

Published by Market Street Books LLC

Copyediting by RainEditing
Production Management by Imdalind Press

Ebook ISBN - 978-1-949725-29-2
Print ISBN - 978-1-949725-32-2
Printed in USA
This Edition, July 2019

CONTENTS

For My Kids

Never Give Up

1

GEMMA

Bombs weren't usually made up of fiery green and lavender blasts. Unless they were made of magic.

Magical blasts of brilliant colors that broke through the walls of banks, jewelry stores, and the occasional clothing store. Whatever we wanted. Today it was a supermarket, one of the fancy ones that the Chosen claimed had healthier food. Healthy, expensive food that they charged twice as much for, while my people, the Undermortals that lived underground, starved.

We may be nothing more than the dirty Drains that they screamed were destroying their perfect world, but I didn't see any reason why that meant we couldn't have the better, more expensive food, too.

Or why we couldn't take it all away from the Chosen and their "Golden" spawn.

It was just there, inside the darkened store, tucked into a complex that had closed for the night. Waiting for us.

I could nearly taste the fresh veg and liquid milk. Cream even. They were all luxuries that would have come from an animal and not from some chemical plant like the rations they would throw at us every week. I had every intention of soaking a bun in the deliciously real, frothy goodness when we got back to the tunnels.

"Ready babe?" Adrian whispered, pressing his chest against my back as his lips tugged at the line of piercings that encircled my ear. His fingers tickled around the black lines of the tattoo that danced around my hip, the heavy ink exposed thanks to a rip in my shirt from the bank heist of last week.

Adrian was forever distracting. It would be so easy to push him back down into the sewer, leave him and his wandering fingers in the dark while I had all the fun. But I needed him, so I would have to deal with the awkward tickling.

Touch was never my favorite, but at least the impending implosion made it more palatable. I could put up with him as long as I got to blow something up.

"Let's make their world burn." A regrettable dimple popped in my smirk as ivy green flame dripped from my fingers, heavy lines of magic splattering over the printed asphalt and eating into it. Boiling it.

Lifting my hand, the magic shot from my palm, fire breaking through the night in a smear of paint against the stars. The blast ripped the doors from the building, breaking the brick and turning it into a shower of rubble the rained over us, filling the last of the night with dust and smoke.

I didn't need the debris to clear in order to know the explosion had worked.

"Go!" I hollered to the clutch of a makeshift army behind me, not like they needed to be told. My people were already running into the building, flashlights blazing, canvas bags opened in preparation.

Eddy, one of the few people I actually trusted, stood by the front door, helping everyone in before he too disappeared through the gnarled fissure of glass and stone. A few of the children who had tagged along were already spray painting our mantra on the debris strewn ground. It was the same scene no matter what we hit, what we stole. Magic, mayhem, and a message. I wasn't even focusing on them anymore. I was already stumbling back into Adrian's waiting arms. The thick corded muscles of his glistening ebony arms wrapped around me, giving me enough support that I wouldn't collapse.

I may have magic, but it was poisoned and illegal and every time I used it, I might as well have been hit by the old train we kept in the tunnels. The old thing was only used as our emergency escape for when the Chosen and their Tarn armies, the CCC, raided the tunnels to exterminate us. Now, I could have sworn the blasted thing was sitting on my chest.

Being the only magic-infected Undermortal may have benefits, destruction and fresh milk above all, but this was not one. Every muscle and bone twisted as though it was going to break, my legs shaking as they attempted to collapse underneath me. Goddamnit. I was better than this, stronger than this. I sure as hell wasn't going to let this pathetic weakness show.

"You okay, Gem?" Adrian tried to hold me closer before he instantly set me back on my feet. He must have heard my teeth grind together, the first sign of the coming bitch-pocalypse.

"Ya." He knew me well enough not to fight me.

Pushing myself away from him, I tried to ignore the ache that was still pulsing through my knees and threatening to pull me to the ground.

I was almost done. One more blast. It would be worth it.

My bad-ass army was now running from the building, laden with bags of food and supplies that they dropped into the sewer drain before vanishing themselves, plunging into the dark that we called home.

"Hurry!" I yelled to the few stragglers in the store, forcing my magic to my fingertips again. The tainted power coursed through my veins, draining what little energy I had left. Adrian's hand was already against my back, helping me to stand, ready for my next collapse. I should probably be more careful with how much power I used, but I didn't care. I wanted them to know we were here.

I wanted them to be afraid.

I wanted them to know what was coming for them.

The bigger the blasts, the brighter the colors. The more they knew.

"I'm the last, Gemma," Eddy yelled as he passed me, his arms absolutely full of flour and yeast. He never got the fluffy white bagged loaves that everyone else did, nor had he wasted too much space on sugary jams that needed refrigeration. Wheat and yeast. Cut and dry. Things we could use for months. Even at eighteen, Eddy was the wisest among us. It was probably why I relied on him so much. We may be nothing more than a few teenage revolutionaries, but between my magic and his logic we were golden. Add in Adrian's brute strength and no one could topple us. I had a few months on the two of them, but even without my magic neither of them would last long if they started treating me like some weak baby.

I could explode more than banks and supermarkets after all.

"We are going to eat for a month after this!" Eddy smiled, although he didn't disappear down the dark sewer drain with everyone else; he turned, eyes smiling as he waited for what was about to happen.

"Kill it, babe," Adrian whispered in my ear, his hands weaving around my sides, gripping my hips and pressing me against him, his heart was an eager hum against my spine.

"Burn little Chosen's, everything will burn," I snarled, lifting my hand and letting the magic that was pooling through my veins erupt in a blast of color, of light, of destruction. Green and gold magic slammed into the front of the store, sending stone, glass, and bits of metal around us as my power ripped through it, destroying the rest of the pretentious building.

The inky black sky was swallowed with an explosion of magic as bright as the most distorted dawn.

Our dawn.

Our future.

"On the second day, I destroyed the night." Screw the Eternals that created this mess. That controlled magic. That blessed and praised the damn Chosen that murdered us.

They weren't the only ones in the world, I would remind them of that.

"Holy hell, Gemma. Don't show off or anything," Eddy snickered as he turned to slip down the drain, Adrian already half-carrying me toward the open manhole. I pushed him away with the force he deserved for trying to coddle me. I could handle a little bit of pain and I could sure as hell walk on my own.

Each stumbling step at a time.

Crackling flames and groaning metal blended with the whine of approaching sirens, the sounds becoming the penultimate theme song for our escape. They sang right along with the mantra we left behind, the red spray paint as much of a promise as it was a warning.

All The Glitters Were Never Gold.

The still wet letters glimmered in the burning dawn, dancing in the night as the lavender of the flames faded, replaced by the spiraling red and blue of their damn cars. The Chosen Council for Community. The CCC.

Armed with weapons and magic alike, they were supposed to protect all of the citizens. Magic. Non-Magic. Everyone was supposed to be safe. They weren't supposed to discriminate.

They did.

What I wouldn't give to get a chance to wring those bastards for all they had done to us. To show them what they were really facing.

I was weak, I was tired, but it would still be worth it. Perhaps I had enough left...

"Not now, babe." I didn't even get a chance to step toward them before Adrian grabbed me, pulling me around and dropping me down the hole to Eddy's waiting arms.

"Nice, Gem," Eddy said as he caught me, his usual snicker echoing over the damp stone. "You're my favorite bad-ass."

"I'm the only bad-ass, Ed." I gave him a wink, and he chuckled, double checking I could stand before setting me into the shallow pools of water that covered the ground.

Eddy's laugh turned into a cackle as Adrian dropped beside us with a grunt and a splash. Sirens and lights were right on top of us now.

"Have enough left?" Red and blue refracted against Adrian's dark features, his eyes narrowed in question in the flashing lights.

"What a ridiculous question." It was also the only way I could get away with not answering him. If I had, the answer would have been a resounding no.

I had used too much magic, and I knew I was going to pay for it. But it was worth it. It always was.

Focusing on the manhole cover, my teeth clamped and ground together as my magic slipped away, pulling it back into place and welding the metal shut. Power dripped from my fingers, everything aching and burning as trickles of blood flowed from my nose.

"Damn it. That's it. Let's get back to Last Pyre. I want to go home," I whispered, letting myself collapse into Adrian, his arms lifting me as he whisked me through the dark. Back to the sewers and the forgotten subway tunnels that was home to us. The Undermortals.

Or as everyone else called us, Drains.

Drains because of where we lived, because of what we were. Because *King* Ilyan and his bastard family, the Eternals, had left us to rot.

Because we lacked magic. Because we were not their precious Chosen. The only ones allowed to have magic, to have power, to have strength.

Well, not anymore. It may have been nothing more than a twist of fate, but I had broken that. I had been bitten by the Vilỳ, the filthy things that awaken the magic in a mortal. One bite, and I had been blessed with the power that was bringing me closer to making the King pay for what he had done.

For all the people he killed.

I would avenge my parents first.

2
___

ROWAN

HE WAS KNOCKING AGAIN.

I knew it was him because there was a special way he had with rapping his knuckles that he had picked up from our Uncle Ryland. Ryland was cool, and when I heard his knock there wasn't a drop of dread associated with it. My oldest brother Talon was a pain in my ass.

"Go away," I yelled toward the door, rolling over and tucking myself further into my bed and all the blankets and pillows that were cluttered over it.

I could burrow all I want, but all it was doing was prolonging the inevitable. You can't keep your irritant of a big brother, and heir to the throne, away for long. Especially when there was magic involved. And Talon had power in spades. That mixed with ego, muscles, and blue eyes that made all the girls swoon. He even looked like Uncle Ryland with his wavy dark hair.

It was no wonder he was quickly becoming the poster boy for our family, 'The Eternals'.

Ridiculously stupid nickname that I was still refusing to adopt.

I was tucked somewhere in the middle of a hugely talented,

successful, and powerful family. The holders of 'the last pure magic on earth', and therefore eternal life. Hence the name. As the third son, I was always lost in Talon's shadow. Which would be a great spot for me to hang out, if the guy would leave me alone.

And he was knocking again. You would think he would have more patience for a guy nearing his sixtieth birthday. But I guess when you always get what you want you don't need to be patient for anything.

"Go away, Talon," I waved my hand through the air and switched the emergency lock closed, fusing the metal latch shut with a tiny bit of heat. Not like it would do anything, I shouldn't have wasted the effort.

Two more knocks and the door swung off its hinges with a blast of hot and cold that swirled through my room and whipped the blankets off my bed. I had stopped sleeping in my boxers years ago for this reason. I had however, forgotten to put a shirt on before crashing last night, or the night before.

Or the night before that.

Who knew? I had been sleeping longer than what one would consider normal, staying awake longer. Something that had been getting worse over the past few years, which was irritating for a few reasons.

"Go away, old man," I grumbled, curling myself into a ball to preserve the last of the heat as the mattress rocked me toward the useless mass that was now bouncing on my bed.

"I wouldn't say that too loud, Atty. Mom and Dad are on their way. You best get moving if you don't want to get 'the look'," Talon even sounded like the heir to a throne. A few years ago some girl in council described his raspy commanding tone as 'sex on a plate' which turned my stomach to this day.

"What's the point? You know she already knows what's going to happen. And don't call me that." I snapped loudly and rolled over, fixing him with my best scowl, he didn't care enough to notice. He was leaning against my headboard with his hands behind his head, looking like an out of place god against the sweaty sheets and mussed blankets.

He was a whole forty years older than me and he didn't look a day over twenty-eight. Oh, the things I had to look forward to as an eternal.

"Why not? It's your name, Atty." I had wasted a scowl on the idiot, the look having earned me a laugh as he ruffled my hair like the grandpa he was. Or would be if he ever found himself a mate and stopped torturing the poor Chosen who saw him for what he was: their ticket to eternal life.

"No, it's not." I rolled out of bed and grabbed one of the dirty shirts from off the floor. Skulls, guns, and roses were emblazoned across the front, but no stains. There was no way my mom was going to let me make my appearance before the start of Imdalind Academy wearing it, but if I could take this last chance to prod her, I was going to do it.

"Rowan Atlas Krul. The king who will carry the world on his shoulders."

"Not a king. And not *Atty*." I was firmly ignoring him now, pulling on socks and making sure my shaggy hair wasn't looking like I had slept for, I checked my phone, two days.

Shit.

I knew I wasn't fooling anyone anymore, but after today I would be out of here, and away from my mom's all-knowing glance. It was a skill of all mothers, but hers was a bit more real. She could literally see the future, and the past, as I was doomed to.

Perhaps she would allow me to continue to pretend this wasn't happening.

That I wasn't becoming like her.

"You're not a king, yet," Talon corrected as if it mattered.

"I'm the third son of two Eternals, Talon. One of which has been in a ruling position since the Renaissance. I'll never be a king, and neither will you."

He shrugged, "Fine with me, I don't mind being *'heir to the throne'*. Ruling would be too much responsibility anyway."

"Less time with the ladies?" I wagged my eyebrows at him as I shrugged on a pair of tight and slightly holey jeans. The style was one that was popular with the mortals, as well as most of the Eternals when we didn't have to go to public functions. Very much not suited for today when we were supposed to appear before thousands of 'our' people leading up to the Gauntlet, and the start of school. But as I have already proved with the shirt, I very much did not give a damn. I had no intention of going anyway, and the clothes were the first step in reminding them all of that.

"Yes, Atty..."

"...Don't call me that..."

"Once you get out of here and to the Academy you'll see what I mean, Rowan." He gave me a wink as I felt the twist of magic flare down the hall from my room. Just feeling them grow closer was gnawing at my stomach and popping a weird warmth up my spine, warmth that I pushed away the same as every other time.

"It's a whole new world outside of these caves."

"I doubt that."

"You don't know what you are missing, Rowan, because you never leave. You hold yourself down here in Imdalind and think this is the world. Dark stone, magic water, and light from a hundred feet above us. But now you have no choice. They will love you. Promise." He bounced off my bed, tousled my hair again and waved his hand in an attempt to fix the door before our parents got here.

One of these days I was going to explain to Talon that love, lust, and resentment were three very different things. Not that he would care. Any attention was good attention in his mind, even if it came from throngs of squealing girls and newly awakened Chosen who would gladly do anything to even be close to one of the Eternals.

I doubted I could do anything to keep them away, which meant I was heading for four years of hell.

Of hiding who, and what, I am, and playing a role, and trying to ignore the fact that the dreams I have every night don't mean something.

That the girl I see every night doesn't mean something.

I had been trying to throw a few extra pairs of shirts in my trunk, but just thinking of her pulled at that warmth in my spine so strongly that my head spun. The magic I worked so hard to keep at bay flared in a flash of red fire, pink hair, and a toothy grin that I had seen far too many times.

Cringing, I pushed the magic away before any prophecy decided to follow along. I really didn't need to slip with Talon here.

Damn Drak magic. I didn't ask for this.

Of all my parents' children, I was the only one to inherit my mother's power. The gift of sight. Of seeing future and past and all the scary powerful magic that came with it. I knew what my mother could do and while there had been a time I wanted it; that time had passed. She was the last Drak on earth. I wasn't interested in being the second.

My eight-year-old sister, Angela, was. She hadn't shown any signs of sight besides one prophetic dream when she was six, however. Besides, she was already struggling to control her power, she didn't need to add this curse to that.

No one did.

I threw the last of shirts in my trunk, well aware that not one of them met the stringent dress code of Imdalind Academy.

One could not live in black dress pants and a white button ups alone. Not for that long.

"Row Row!" Angela's shriek preceded a grunt from Talon and the clatter of what was clearly wood splintering against stone.

So much for fixing the door. Angela had made quick work of Talon's patch job.

"Hey, Angie!" She launched herself at my back, nearly pulling me down on top of the partially packed trunk. I swung her around, holding her against me with ease. Wrestling two older brothers all my life was good for some things.

And tickling the crap out of my baby sister was the biggest among them.

"You gonna miss me?" I taunted, digging my fingertips into her ribs and the soft flesh under her arms, sending her squealing.

"Hey! No! Let me go!" She gasped, her writhing picking up as the tickling did.

"Not until you tell me how much you are going to miss me." More tickling, more taunting, all of it highlighted by my mom's laughter right behind me. "How much are you going to miss me?"

"I'm... gonna... I'm... Stop!" She couldn't even form the full sentence. Perfect. Which of course meant time for more tickling.

"How much are you gonna miss me, Angie?" I asked, throwing her over my shoulder as I attacked the backs of her knees. Unfortunately, that also put her in prime position to pound her little fists against my back.

"Mercy! I'll miss you! Let me down, Row!" Her shrieks had reached an apex and while I didn't drop her, I did stop the onslaught by holding her against me in one of my favorite Angie

Bear hugs. The smell of magic in her hair was like spring and sandalwood.

Assaulting. Perfect.

My heart clenched. There was little I would miss in the dratted caves we called home. Angie was at the top of that list.

"So, tell me why you aren't joining us for the Gauntlet?" Mom was already giving me a look.

This was how most conversations went with my powerfully confident mother, diving right in as though any discussion was half way through, mostly because she had already seen the first part.

She stood, dressed in some weird pantsuit number that didn't fit her personality at all. She always wore jeans with as many holes as I did, some weird graphic on her shirts. Dad, however, was always a King, always regal and kind and currently smiling down on me with his usual 'I'm so proud of you I might explode' expression.

My parents were polar opposites in a lot of ways, appearance was one.

My dad was tall, with blonde hair that fell half way down his back. My mother's hair was just as long, but dark and wavy. All of their hair was braided as a sign of bonded mates, but my parents' braids were intertwined with the long golden ribbon that served as their crown. His eyes were the sky blue that at one point had denoted the royal family, which is why all my uncles had them. And most of my siblings.

And by most, I really mean all of them but me. Because I needed another thing to add to the 'ways I don't fit into my family' list. Their eyes were blue, mine were a deep mossy green. My mother swore that was the color of her eyes before she had received her bite from the Vilÿs and became a Chosen, but it wasn't helping. Her silver eyes were almost as famous as her Drak abilities.

Which I am pretty sure I already mentioned I was refusing to inherit.

Mom gave me a look, making it clear she was going to pull the answer out of me if I didn't start talking. This was really not how I had planned this conversation to go.

"I'm not going to the Gauntlet because it's a foolish tradition that has hindered an entire race of people for over a century." Luckily, I didn't even have to think about the answer. I did, however, turn away, running my fingers through my shaggy black hair. Maybe I could get her to switch subjects and start pressuring me to cut it again.

"Geeze, Atty, you sound like Dad." Thanks Talon. We clearly needed his snotty perspective on this.

I turned, shooting him a look from where he was lounging on my bed again. Great. I had planned to take that pillow and now it had his greasy curls all over it.

"Well then, Dad and I sound like logic," I snapped, pulling the pillow out from under him and throwing the thing in the top of my trunk, closing and locking the ancient case with a snap.

"I agree with you, Rowan, and with your father. That's why we have taken steps to reverse the damage that was done. Unity and equality has been our goal from the beginning, and it's time we got back on track." Mom didn't need to say the next part in order for me to hear it. She had said it enough.

'Which is why it is important that we all go and make a unified front.'

It was the same argument she had been making for weeks.

I agreed with her, and I agreed with what was happening, but I also knew that me showing my face on that raised platform with everyone else was going to create the worst start possible for the next four years.

Rowan the Prince, at Imdalind Academy.

I had kept myself out of the public eye for multiple reasons.

First, my Drak blood kept me sleeping in weird cycles. Second, I didn't need to go to the damn school. I already knew how to use my magic. Third, I was being forced to attend specifically as a show of faith for the royal family, as some regal representative. I wasn't interested in the title or the job.

This monarchy had caused enough problems.

"You can do that without me being there, mom. I've agreed to go to the damn school, isn't that enough for you?" I was working very hard to keep both tone and temper under control. I could already feel both pressing under the surface, prodding my magic into a boil.

"Are we changing the name to 'That Damn School'? I like it, not sure Cail will approve, but, I vote yes!" The new voice pulled into the room as my other older brother, Dramin stepped over the rubble of my former door to join us, his tall frame, blue eyes, and blonde hair a frightening replica of our father.

I would gladly welcome Dramin and his wife, Patrice, into my room over my idiot eldest brother any day, but this was getting ridiculous.

"Is everyone and their dog coming to see me off?" I tried not to sound too hysterical. Instead, I snapped, my magic flaring and causing the locks on my trunk to flick open and earning me a look from my dad, his eyes narrowing.

Yeah, I know. I should watch my temper.

"Don't flatter yourself, Row," Dramin said calmly. "You aren't that special. We are all here for the Gauntlet, but I'll give you a hug anyway."

"The Gauntlet?" I scoffed, the nape of my neck prickling as I dodged Dramin's open arms and wide grin and pushed the magic away. "Since when does that race need the full family present?"

"More like the full guard," Patrice answered, her voice as soft as her husbands.

"It's the anniversary race. We are changing everything..."

"And not expecting the outcome to go over well." My mother and father spoke in turns, a simple logical answer. I probably would have believed it too if they weren't all shuffling their feet.

I looked between them all, waiting for someone to answer, their dark looks weren't giving me a lot of confidence.

"Something happened didn't it?" The powerful Drak magic was eating into the nerves at the base of my neck now, the wicked side eye everyone was passing around making it hard to ignore.

"There was another attack last night. A grocery store down in the low district, near the water line, sometime after midnight. Only basics were taken and the building was destroyed. We are sure it is the Undermortals."

Undermortals. The poor people who had retreated to living underground rather than deal with the Chosen, the Tarns, and the Mortals who still play into this royal facade. There were more Undermortals than Mortals now. I understood why.

I had seen why.

Mothers eyes dug into mine, the tickling power in my neck swelling. I pushed it away, not that mattered. I knew what I would see.

Her.

I swallowed. It wasn't the first time I had questioned if I should tell them what I had seen. Tell them about her. But telling them would be the end of denying what was happening. I wouldn't be able to hide the magic anymore.

Besides, something about her felt like it was only for me.

"Are you sure it's wise to continue with our plan if these attacks are coming from the Undermortals?" Dramin asked. "That's what... ten in the last two months?"

"That we know of. But the buses have already been dispatched to the communities we have been able to identify, and I don't see anything coming. Our plan is still safe." Mom turned to me again, giving me the same look. Digging into my soul, or into my sight.

God, I hated when she did that. I quickly busied myself with straightening my already packed trunk.

"Either someone came in contact with a loose Vilỳ and has un-centered magic, or they have figured out how to build a bomb that mimics it."

Even I didn't have the answer to that, and I had been dreaming of her and her Undermortal community for years.

The despair, the starvation. I saw more than a fair share of tears. I cried with her, even if she hadn't known.

I saw what we had done to them. Inviting a few hundred to run the Gauntlet, get magic and enroll in school wasn't going to help anything.

"I still think it's a bomb," Talon cut mom off, all business now. "The Vilỳ's have been captured since before I was born, there is no way those Drains could have--"

"Watch your language, Talon. We don't use that word, as I have explained before," my father roared, Talon wilting underneath his scorn before he turned back to me. I could have sworn the air turned to ice.

Talon had sure frozen like it did.

"Rowan, I understand you are upset about the situation, and I know that what is happening is not your ideal situation. But it is the ideal for the thousands under our command that need us right now. That all begins today, with the Gauntlet, and we need to show all of them that we are unified in this decision."

If you ever need to feel what it's like to be properly scolded, try having a dad that is both immortal and king. I could feel his displeasure in my toes, his voice rumbling in the old Czech language that only our family really used anymore.

Guess I wasn't the only one fighting a temper today. If I had inherited one thing from my dad, it was that. A fiery temper worthy of a few legends and a dozen stories. He, however, never lost control of his magic. It wasn't something anyone else in my family did. We were better than that, or supposed to be.

"Bringing more of the mortals into the school isn't going to help, though. It's going to segregate lines further. We have to heal them before we can join them..." I didn't get much further before he cut me off with one sharp stare.

"This is the first step, Rowan. I fought for centuries for peace and equality. We won't let some parading Chosen's upset a culture and a power that should benefit all. We have not forgotten the Undermortals. We have been working for years to realign our society. You are a big part of that."

"I don't need to be your poster boy, dad. If you need someone there, send Wyn... or Talon! Everyone loves them."

"Atty's right," Talon began, and I swear I almost punched him. "Everyone loves me."

Yep, totally going to punch him.

"You should get on the train, Row," he taunted, winking at me as I fumed. "Maybe people will love you too. Well, like, but even that would be a step up."

That time the lid to my trunk flew open, sending pillow, shirts, and a few pairs of underwear over everyone. Poor Angie's eyes grew wider at the display, more for the underwear than the yelling. The yelling had become the norm.

"Shut the fuck up, Tal." Thankfully Dramin was on my side, didn't derail me from my sudden need for violence.

Too bad I didn't get more than a few steps before the swimming sensation at the back of my neck fizzled down my spine and I was forced to a halt, snapping my eyes shut and doing everything I could to force the magic away.

Great, now my mom was looking at me too. She clearly felt the sight trying to pull its way into me. And now my parents were doing that thing where they talked into each other's mind, giving each other shifty side eyes that they were still convinced no one noticed.

"Can you guys please not do that, just for today, just for right now?"

I would seriously give anything to go live amongst the Undermortals right now, find that girl that keeps trying to take over my sights... I mean dreams, and figure out what her deal is. Not be magic. Not be royal. Not deal with this.

"Why don't you all give us a minute?" My mom cut in before anyone else could open their mouths. Everyone shuffled out, but not before putting me on the receiving end of every single guilty stare known to man.

Well, all except Dramin. The guy was so easy going he was probably going to go find our Uncle Thom so they could stare at a wall together and make jokes that only they could understand.

Mom didn't waste a minute in repairing and securing the door after everyone had left, the lock snapping into place and flaring what little control I had.

This was not going to end well.

"You slept for two days that time."

Yes, mom, I know. I wasn't going to answer her. Instead, I went back to repacking my trunk, going extra slow and doing it the mortal way.

"And four days last week. Did you sleep at all between that?"

No, no mom I didn't. Good thing she couldn't hear my thoughts like she could hear dads.

"You know I can't force you to do anything. I won't force you to drink Black Water again, or see. But I don't think you can ignore it any longer, Rowan. I couldn't stop--"

"I can stop it." I was firm. I didn't want to talk about it, that first time still haunted me. I still woke up in a cold sweat from those nightmares.

It was ten years ago that I held that mug in my hands, but my choice hadn't changed. I never wanted to see that again. I never wanted to see anything.

Maybe it was desperation, panic, hope. I didn't know. But I would squash that dangerous power down until it didn't exist anymore.

"Then I will trust you. We need to be a unified front in this Rowan. I am glad you are choosing--" I gave her a look, "*complying* to enroll in the school this year. Having you there in our stead will help us to heal the wounds your father and I are trying to mend in our people--"

"You sound like dad, too." I didn't turn, I just threw another pair of boxers in my trunk and smashed my pillow on top of it. Packing the mortal way really didn't do much in the way of efficiency.

She chuckled with the lighthearted sound she always had, another thing I would probably miss. If only because I knew she wasn't laughing at me. She really did sound like dad.

"I hope you find the answers you need, Row. But I can't send you off like this." She cut herself short, stepping behind me and placing a large earthen mug on my dresser. The ugly thing sitting in the mirror as both the mug and its reflection stared at me. I jerked up, meeting the silver eyes of my mother in the mirror.

"I know you don't accept what's inside you, but there might come a time when you can't ignore it. There might come a time that you need it."

"What did you see mom?" I recognized that tone in her voice far too well.

"Take the mug, Rowan. You'll know when you need it. You'll know when to trust her. You'll know how to use it." She smiled at me through the mirror, her hand soft on my shoulder as her magic buzzed between us, one last touch before she turned toward the door, the long golden ribbon from her intricate braid trailing behind her.

"We will come and gather you after the Gauntlet, Rowan. You are doing the right thing."

And she was gone, leaving me with her last few words that were as confusing as pretty much everything else she said. That and an ugly earthen mug made from the magic dirt in the wells of Imdalind that lay far below the caves that served as our castle.

A massive pool of water, surrounded by mud that together created the key source of power, food, and sight for a Drak.

I wanted nothing more than to chuck the thing across the room and watch as it shattered into a million pieces.

Instead I tucked it under the pillow in my trunk, closed and latched the lid, and went back to bed.

3

GEMMA

Mornings after a raid always hurt. Everything was too splintered and broken for me to do much more than roll over with a groan, prod Adrian awake and beg him to bring me food while I crawled myself to the old marble tiled room that had once upon a time been a functioning bathroom.

I would drag myself through dozens of makeshift beds, cursing the demon bird that bit me, swearing at anyone who got in my way, and whining about wanting to go back to sleep.

"Holy shit. Damn demon bird!" I hadn't even rolled out of bed, and I was already cursing to the sky.

That was two check marks crossed off my list at it hadn't been five minutes. Today was going to be a doozy.

Aches rattled every bone, veins pulsing with my usual magical hangover. I had experienced both types and I definitely preferred the one you got after drinking too much of Eddy's fermented soup.

One roll toward the overprotective hunk who fancied himself my boyfriend and it was clear two things were wrong.

It wasn't morning, and Adrian was about to be in a world of pain.

His nest of blankets was empty. In fact, every cot and lean-to directly around me was empty. I didn't see one dirty head or happily chatting child as they tried to steal a third bun from the stores. There wasn't one whisper from the plotting pre-teens who were already too thirsty for the revolution to begin.

The entire room that was usually bustling with Undermortals was empty.

Rumor was that the tunnels had once been a huge hub for travelers that were hustling to work, or to another city or country on something the elders called 'validations'. That was all from a world that was long forgotten, however. All that meant nothing around here anymore.

Trains were gone, the travelers only existed in shadows and the jagged colorful artwork that covered the tunnel walls in a language no one knew anymore. Yellow tiled mosaics were everywhere, the cracked things shifting and twisting in fragile designs that I used to pretend were some kind of prophecy for the new world to come.

Fairy stories from a kid too full of hope. That was a decade ago, before I was bitten and knocked unconscious for six months. Now I knew better. Any future with flowers and sunshine was something we would have to make, something we would have to kill for.

If the CCC and the Tarns didn't kill us first.

Please don't let that be what happened here.

The Protectors can't have raided the tunnel so soon. They can't have tracked us down so fast, there were simply too many Undermortal camps littered in the web of underground tunnels for them to have zeroed in on us. Even if they had, leaving me behind made no sense. It's not like I exactly blended into the sea of brown blankets with my bright pink mohawk, lines of silver piercings in my ears, and so many tattoos on my arms you could barely see the olive skin anymore. I did that specifically so they would notice me, and here I was being left behind.

This was clearly Adrian's fault. He was supposed to be my bodyguard or something. Although after one drunken night of sharing the same bed he seems to have other plans. Sleep with the guy once and it all goes to his head.

Rage flooded my veins as I pulled myself to sit. My magic flared at the motion, thankfully taking away a bit of the morning after aches. I was in serious need of a stiff drink. I'd grab one on the way to the ass kicking I was sure to find closer to the MidCity hall that served as our main meeting hall. And where a booming voice was now echoing from.

Deep. Dangerous. And followed by a particularly high giggle.

"What the hell?" I didn't hold back, I yelled so loud my frustration rattled the rat cages that hung from the ceiling. CandleEars, my grandmother had called them once. The world before the war had ridiculous names for things.

I slid around, pulling on the shiny black pair of combat boots I had stolen a few months ago and jumped to stand.

And went right back down.

"Shit!"

There was the ache I had been expecting.

"Having some trouble?" Eddy's familiar chuckle echoed from the opening of the hall, the dark tattoo of a snake on his arms folded over a grungy shirt that was emblazoned with what he swore was a cartoon character from two hundred years ago, before the war. Eddy was obsessed with that crap.

"Where is everyone?" I pushed myself to stand again, taking two shaky steps before pushing away his offer to help. "And why the hell did you leave me here?"

"I wasn't about to drag you by your feet around the place. You know how you get after a raid. Everyone's in MidCity.

Something happened. A good something." He tacked on that last part when I opened my mouth in preparation to rage at him.

"You mean besides the fact that we knocked over a store and brought home enough food to feed everyone in Last Pyre, SafeHome, and probably Fire Fate for a month. You're welcome." I folded my arms and leaned against the slimy stone of the annex tunnel, taking the opportunity to catch my breath.

"Yes, something is happening in Imdalind."

Normally, that phrase would be accompanied by a terrifying tale of one of the Undermortal communities being raided. Or some speech from the damn King's brother, Ryland who liked to dictate everyone's life. But Eddy was still smiling, and that infernal giggling was still pouring from the main hall.

I lifted a brow in question, but the loon kept grinning, waiting for me to ask him. What did he think, he was that delusional Queen who had everyone thinking she could see the future? Seeing as he wasn't going to divulge on his own, I pushed past him and charged my destination to the heightening voices.

"Aren't you going to ask what happened?" Eddy asked with his usual chuckle, catching up to me.

"No." I kept walking, heavy soles slapping in time with the laugh that had started to grate against my spine.

Laughing was not unheard of, but laughing because of something in Imdalind or those damn Eternals that ruled us all was pretty much the unspoken rule number one of 'things you didn't do in Last Pyre'. Someone was breaking my rules.

Sore muscles and fiery veins be damned, I sprinted up the stairs to MidCity, the junction that connected Last Pyre to several surrounding communities. The people I had unofficially led for the last two years mixed with the Undermortals from Safe Home, and Fire Fate that usually came to help us with the raids. Their community tattoos, a lock in the shape of a heart and a bloody scythe respectively, intermingled with the burning wand of my people, making it hard to tell who was who. Judging by the numbers, everyone who had helped with the raid last night had gone home and brought people back with them. The air was dripping with excitement. The talking, laughing masses clustered around five white buses, each one emblazoned with the seal of that goddamned academy.

A dragon, a weird mug, something that looked like tree roots, and the sparks of what I was sure magic was supposed to look like. It was the dumbest, and ugliest, thing. Which was fitting seeing as it was for the dumbest, and ugliest school.

The one I would gladly burn to the ground if I got the chance.

"Fucking Imdalind Academy."

The place was a massive institution in the middle of what used to be Europe. At least that's what the rumors say. No one had actually been able to find it, and plenty of Undermortals had tried. You have to be taken there, probably by those damn Eternals àfter you run their damn Gauntlet and win a place at the school. The school was where Chosen trained and perfected their magic, so that they could become powerful and grow up and lord over us. Then they would all get married and have their glistening Golden children that they would raise to run the Gauntlet, go to school, and train to keep murdering and beating us down, just like the generations of Chosen before them.

An endless cycle.

Prejudiced. Destructive. Murderers.

Winning the Gauntlet was the only way to get a bite from a Vilỳ, gain magic and become Chosen. The Goldens who win become Chosen, the ones who don't are Tarnished and reduced to little more than servants. Angry, vindictive little things who would stop at nothing to regain the approval of their society. Some of them ended up below ground with us after they failed to receive their mark. But most of them remained above ground, The Tarns.

A whole fucking system revolving around ugly little birds and their magical bite. Which was why the Eternals controlled all the Vilỳ's by hiding them in the Gauntlet.

Control the Vilỳ's and you control the magic.

Well, until me.

Their dumb little plan had been broken by one tiny winged man-like thing with the face of a demon and fangs as long as a finger. The monster had been missed in the sweeps two hundred years ago, one creature with gnashing teeth and a hunger for human blood that I had found hiding in a collapsed tunnel inside of what used to be Prague.

I wasn't even ten yet. They nearly left me for dead. Would have if my mother wasn't so stubborn. But that's a sob story for another life.

I was over it.

Instinctively, I pulled my holy jean jacket down over my left forearm, not that anyone could see the ugly raised brand where the rat had bitten me. It was always hidden, nestled between tattoos and a scar from when I had tried to cut the thing out once, just above my elbow. If you didn't know what you were looking for, it looked more like some of the scars you see in the elders from when we used to hunt the larger rats in the flooded tunnels.

It didn't matter, though, I wasn't about to take chances, not with Chosen bastards lingering around the damn vans and staring at us so darkly I couldn't tell if they were scared, or one step away from murdering us all.

"What in the hell is this nonsense about?" I didn't even try to keep my voice low, the disgust flying as I stepped into the crowd, pulling the focus of quite a few of the eager Undermortals.

Eager.

What the hell?

My stomach turned, my pathetically weak body threatening to turn out the contents completely. That look should never be associated with that school. Or with any Chosen. For all we knew it was another ploy to round us all up. Take us to The Wastelands, the work camps near the burned out parts of the old Med Sea that weren't quite as poisoned with radiation.

"Baby, you're awake. Just in time," Adrian burst through the crowd, his arms wide as he attempted to sweep me up. Like hell if I was going to let that happen with all these people watching.

"Answers first, affection later." Thank god he stepped back; I didn't want to have to throw him there. "What's going on?"

"It's our chance, baby." I gave him a look, not like it would stop him from calling me that.

"Chance for what? Lifelong servitude and radiation poisoning?"

"Not unless that lifelong servitude comes with a chance to make that evil overlord of a King drown in his own blood," Adrian whispered, leaning into me until he could tug at the rip in my t-shirt.

I jerked away, but not at the touch.

We had been talking about our grand finale for years, imagining what it would be like to end the Eternals and all of the royal family, show them what they had done before we killed them. I had never killed anyone before, I was saving my first one for them.

I highly doubted that it could be so close, or that they would send comfortable transportation to get us there.

"You've lost your mind, Adrian," I said with too much snarl, pushing myself away from his searching fingers.

"Not quite, Gem. They are filling those buses, taking Undermortals to the Gauntlet," Eddy provided as he came up behind us.

Adrian tried to sweep me up again, but I flattened my palm against his chest, holding him back as one spark of yellow magic jumped between my fingertips.

Dangerous considering our surroundings. But none of the Chosen that were chatting with my people could see past their false smiles anyway.

"They are letting us run the Gauntlet? They are letting us into that damn school?"

"Technically they were always supposed to, weren't they?" Ed mused with a smile and a hand through his ruddy hair. "Not that we could get passed the Tarn armies to get there."

"Don't tell me you've tried, Ed." I shot Eddy a fiery look that shut him up pretty darn fast.

"It's the seventieth anniversary of the damn race," Adrian provided, his hand weaving around my waist. I was too focused on the vans to pull away that time.

"The seventieth anniversary of tyranny and persecution against Undermortals, you mean." I was having trouble controlling the power that was flooding my veins now, little sparks were spewing from underneath my fingertips, warming the palms of my hands as I pressed them against my spiked leather belt.

"They are celebrating, Gemma," Adrian continued, pulling me into him, resting his chin against my shoulder as we watched the Chosen. "They are celebrating by letting us come try our hand at the Gauntlet. Letting us try to get our own magic. And they are doing it by sending us into the race with the precious children of every Chosen in the world. All those Golden brats, in one place. Mortal. Unprotected..."

His low tone was a seduction that rattled against my spine, my stomach twisting in need and lust. Although that might have been more from what was coming; from what was already forming in my mind.

"And ready to see how tarnished their glittering world really is," I finished for him.

"*All The Glitters Were Never Gold.*" We whispered in unison. Eddy let out a low bellied laugh, the sound following me as I strode forward, right to the bulky Chosen in front of the nearest van. He had hair the color of thatch, his magic bright and nearly as oppressive as his size. He was smiling at three girls in front of him, balancing a playing card on the tip of his finger, hearts and diamonds spinning end over end.

"I want to run the Gauntlet," I interrupted confidently, causing both his card to fall and every head in the immediate area to turn. "I want a chance to show the Eternals what our people can do. What we can *really* do."

I smiled brightly, clearly taking the words right out of his mouth. He looked like he had been slapped with his jaw wagging like that.

"Why is that so shocking?"

"It's not. We had expected to fill these buses in minutes, but no one has been interested. Your kind should feel so blessed for even a chance to have even a portion of what we have."

It was taking everything in me not to rise, not to let my magic smack him into his damn bus and curl the thing around him. Later. Right then, I needed to save my strength.

"You just needed to ask the right person."

I didn't smile, I didn't wait for him to snarl one more degrading comment, I stepped onto the bus, walking right to the back and to the padded seats that were filled with as many lies as they were stuffing.

That was all it took for my people, for the army I had built, to fall into place.

Hundreds of Undermortals followed me on board in lines, the pierced, tattooed hoards the Chosen found so disgusting piling three and four deep into rows that were meant to fill half that.

We sat in the aisles, threw open the windows in the hope of finding more space, and cleared the platform in what felt like seconds. The five Chosen drivers were left looking dumbfounded. Mr. Card Trick's jaw was sagging again.

"Exactly what are you planning?" Eddy whispered as he sat beside me, Adrian taking the seat on the other side of the aisle.

"Like you said, it's the seventieth anniversary. I think they are going to be needing some fireworks."

4

———

SIA

"Name?"

The haggard old lady behind the desk didn't even glance up from her computer. She continued clicking on the sleek, metallic mouse, the electronic card game she was playing reflecting in her overly large, and overly thick glasses.

No wonder this line was taking so long. Suzan, according to her nametag, wasn't even paying attention.

I should be mad, but I had been waiting for this day for seventeen years. Too long to get pissed at some Tarn and get myself kicked out only moments before the Gauntlet was to begin. Besides, Suzan had clearly come from a Chosen family like myself. She was too clean and had none of the tattoos or piercings that the Drains usually covered themselves in.

We were equals, for now. Goldens. Children of the Chosen, raised in the gleaming world of magic. I was sure she had entered the Gauntlet as I was about to do. The clean, unmarked skin on her wrists made it clear she hadn't succeeded.

She hadn't received a kiss from the Vilỳ, the winged magical beast whose poison awakens the magic in a mortal. She was never blessed with magic. She was nothing more than a Tarnished Golden now. A Tarn.

I was not going to meet the same fate.

"Sia Demarco." I spoke my name slowly, confidently, just as my father had demanded of me my entire life. It made little difference. My agitation boiled into a steam when she didn't click right over from her game.

"Daughter of Samantha and Giovanni Demarco." I tacked that last part on for effect, pushing my sheet of chestnut hair behind me as if that alone would catch her attention.

Suzan froze, but not from the glittering strands of hair that my mother had bewitched that morning. She recognized my parents' names.

Of course she did.

My parents were some of the most prominent Chosen in our area. My father had campaigned for the imprisonment and reuse of the Drains for years. Obsolete mortals were useless to the world and needed to be dealt with after all. They were drains of society, living in the abandoned drains of the world. Last year, my mother had led the efforts to clear the old subway tunnels they called home. Which, if I had to guess, was where the Tarn that was sitting beside the useless Suzan had come from. Thick black lines of the tattoo on his neck were practically bursting out of the makeup he was attempting to use to cover it. Most of the Tarns who failed the Gauntlet chose to hide underground. Ashamed.

Suzan hadn't chosen that path. She should be commended for choosing to serve those better than herself. She had chosen to make herself useful to those above her.

I gave her a brighter smile.

"Demarco," she repeated. There was a bit of hostility in her voice as she finally looked up from the screen, fixing me with a steely grey stare from behind her grubby spectacles. I didn't let my smile falter. "Come to join your parents in their blessings of power?"

"No," I said, leaning closer to her and putting my hands flat on the folding table they were using for check-ins. "I've come to surpass them."

She flinched. My smile stretched.

"Well, I hope it works out for you. Everyone here has the same goal after all. Only the best will see the end." She gave me a narrow stare before clicking a few things on her screen and handing me a small steel blade, a cracked rock, a canvas bag, and an old laminated sheet of instructions. I didn't need any of it. My father had prepared me better than that. I took it anyway, giving her a simpering smile.

"May the wells of Imdalind follow your quest," she recited the line at the same time as the Tarn next to her. Echoes of the deadpanned greeting banged through the noise of all the Gauntlet runners lined up behind me.

"You can count on it." My smile did not falter as she sent me on my way. I passed the security check and stepped into the old train station that they had used for the Gauntlet since they caught the last of the Vilẏs two hundred years ago and the Queen had started the school.

My school.

My heart was an absolute hum as I ascended the steps, staring at the chipped gargoyles that flagged the massive carved doors like sentinels. The first gatekeepers toward gaining my mark.

Every surface in the massive wood and marble lobby glistened with magic after having been scrubbed clean by the Chosen workers last night. Not that it made any difference with the wall of bodies and odor that now flooded it. I had been prepared for the hundreds of Goldens who would gather to fight for their place to follow their parents in a path of magic, but there were far too many of the vile sewer dwellers here than I had been warned about.

They may be allowed to run the Gauntlet, but it was useless. They would never win; they were only serving to overwhelm the air with their stench. They were wasting everyone's time by being here.

The canvas bag was good for something, I guess. I balled the thing up and smashed it against my nose, staring at the group of Drains that were nervously hovering to my left.

Scared, pathetic little sewer rats. They weren't welcome here, and I would do my best to make sure they knew that.

Maybe the knife would be good for something.

Noxious fumes dampened; I reached the edge of the crowd as my name rang over the nervous buzz of voices in a high-pitched squeal. Tasha. Only one person could make a sound like that. It wasn't even worth turning to her. She would catch up with me. I was too busy pushing my way past the others; who might as well be sightseers with how they were staring at the mosaic on the ceiling with their jaws sagging open.

"Idiots! We are here to win, not to ogle." I pushed some Drain with a bubblegum-pink mohawk aside, earning myself a glare from the snarly girl who had marred her face with a few too many piercings. Fecking Drains. I could already tell she was not going to survive this. No muscle. No training. Too foul. Moving on.

"You don't want to go that way," Tasha said in a sing song tone as she reached me, wrapping her hand around my arm and pulling me back. "It's a madhouse that way, Sia."

"But that's where my father says the best starting point is. It has to be this way." I pulled my arm out of her grip, ready to continue my charge through the crowd, but she pulled me back again, her sharp nails digging into my skin.

I cringed and stepped back, massaging my arm.

She was as ruthless as I was.

This is how I knew Tasha and I were going to be the first through the gates, and the first to receive a bite. We had trained for this since we were small. For the Gauntlet, for magic; all of it.

The magic of the Chosen didn't pass on through generations like it did for the Eternals. My grandparents and my parents all ran and won the Gauntlet, my great-grandparents having been bitten in the war before. We were meant for this power. Meant for this world.

But, I could do better than that. I would be the first to get a bite in this race, enroll in Imdalind Academy, and find myself an Eternal to take as a mate and give me the eternal life and magic that I really deserved. I already had everything planned out.

"We can't deviate from the plan, Tash." I was ready to pull her after me if I had to. "This is what we planned on and I won't let anything stand in my way."

"How about anyone? Ryland and Cail have decided to set up shop up there. There is no way you are getting through."

That smug little laugh in her voice said it all. I gave her a look, but she only smiled and nodded towards a raised platform where three Eternals were standing.

Ryland, Mira, and Cail stood on a large stage; waving, chatting, and laughing with some of the runners. Hundreds more were pushing up behind them as they tried to get closer to the Eternals, hands outstretched in the hope of a touch.

These weren't the Skřítek guard of the Eternals. Ryland was the brother of the King, Mira his wife. Their nephew Cail served as the headmaster of Imdalind Academy.

They all appeared the same as they had my entire life.

Young, gorgeous, tall, and powerful. As Eternals, they did not age. Even though these three were some of the younger Eternals that guarded over Imdalind; Ryland having recently celebrated his three hundredth birthday, they didn't look a day over thirty. What an amazingly handsome thirty it was.

The other Eternals, although older, were the same. The King, Ilyan Krul, was easily a few thousand years old. Wynifred Krul, the King's sister-in-law, was not much younger.

It made sense that the majority of the Eternals and the royal family that ruled over all with magic were related. Of course, it all stemmed from one man who had enough children to create an army. Which is exactly what he tried to do, and what Ilyan and his wife, Joclyn, had stopped.

Which is what made Mira a god to so many. She was bitten when the Vilỳ rampaged the earth, as my grandparents had been. She had survived the bite, and she and Ryland met and fell in love. My father said there was more to the story than that, but I didn't care. All that mattered was that a Chosen had mated an Eternal and she had gained eternal life.

Seeing her on that platform was a good omen to my success.

"Let's pick another door," Tasha whined, pulling me out of the childlike awe that had crippled me. "There is no point in going that way."

"You mean, Tash, that there is no way I am going to miss it." I gave her a wink, and she rolled her eyes, although it was half-hearted. She clearly expected this to happen and didn't even fight me as I dragged her through the crowd toward the platform.

The closer we got, the better I could see them. Right down to Cail's dark eyes, and each curl in Ryland's brown-black hair. Mira was as beautiful and strong as I had imagined her. She may not be as tall as the boys, but it didn't matter, you could barely tell with the confidence that shown from her grey eyes. Her long blonde hair was braided in the long strands of mating only the Eternals used. Her chunky jewelry and elegant style was something I had modeled my own after, having cut and pinned every picture I had found of her in magazines for years.

It was the power in her eyes that was impacting me the most, though. She had worked as Ryland's bodyguard, his second, long before they were mated. She was watching everyone now and it was clear she wasn't missing anything.

"God, she's such a badass!" Tasha said from behind me as I continued to plow our way forward. She had taken the words right out of my mouth. I would meet her someday, didn't matter who I had to kill to get there.

Now, however, I forced myself to look away and continued muscling our way toward the entrance my dad had sworn would give us the upper hand. Just as I looked away, the crowd went crazy. Screaming. Yelling. Girls jumped up and down as they pressed against us.

The Gauntlet couldn't have started already. I had planned to get there an hour early so I had enough time to get to my place, but not enough time that I would be fatigued from standing. They weren't pushing us toward the entrance, however, they were pushing us toward the platform.

"Oh my! It's Ilyan!" I had no idea who had spoken, but it didn't matter. The crowd was turning into a mob and now I knew why.

Ryland and Cail had been little more than pre-show entertainment. Ilyan and Joclyn were here, and they were the main act. The immortal king and his once mortal queen, stood in the center of the platform as regal and perfect as they always were. The golden ribbons of their crowns wound through their hair, twisting around one another as though they were caught in a breeze. I had never seen them this close before. Not many had. They normally sent Ryland to handle appearances. With the screaming and clamoring that was happening, it was clear why.

It grew significantly worse when Talon burst his way out to stand next to his father.

Talon was Ilyan and Joclyn's oldest son, and heir to the throne. He was in his late fifties now, and I had never seen anyone hotter. God. I, along with every other girl here wanted to lick him, and we were all screaming loud enough to say so. Well... they were. I stood, the lone smiling girl in the sea of screamers. Talon noticed me immediately and smiled. It took everything in me not to lose it along with the rest of them, a necessary decorum which only got harder to control when Talon's younger siblings followed him onto the platform.

Dramin and his wife Patrice walked into the center of the stage, along with the youngest of all the Eternals; eight-year-old Angela.

I wasn't the first to notice that someone was missing.

Rowan, the third son to the King and Queen, was nowhere to be seen. He was a few months older than me, and was to attend Imdalind Academy this year. The year of his nineteenth birthday, as his siblings had done before him. You could only run the Gauntlet between the ages of seventeen and nineteen, and I had even waited a year so I could enroll in the academy the same year that Rowan would be there.

He was the reason I was going to win the Gauntlet. He was the reason I had done everything. To get his attention, his heart and his hand. And he wasn't there.

Everything tensed at the possibility that something was wrong. Rumors had been swirling about his health for years; many saying that he was born with too much of his mother's mortality and his magic was damaging him. I certainly hoped that wasn't true.

"Where's Rowan?" Screams and shouts echoed around me, but I still did not rise; other than to give Tasha one quizzical lift of my brow. She shrugged and went back to making a fool of herself and screaming like a madman.

Ilyan stepped forward, pulsing his hands down as though he was fanning the crowd. Waves of hot and cold moved through the air with each beat of his hands. Numbing our minds, stilling our tongues and pulling us all into quiet. His mouth did not move as his magic washed over the room. A spark of power never dripped from his fingertips as you saw with the Chosen. His power just existed. It ran over all of us in a pressurized weight until everything was calm. I had never seen magic like that before. I didn't know it was possible.

But King Ilyan was an Eternal. He was the king.

"Thank you for the warm welcome," Ilyan said in an accent that rumbled through the air with its own kind of power. "We will be beginning the challenge in a few moments. I, and my family, are proud to join you for this, the seventieth anniversary of this competition. We are proud of the Chosen that have wielded the magic of Imdalind since we first began this challenge, and are eager to welcome more into Imdalind at the completion of this race."

"Where's Rowan?" A shout broke over the King's speech, causing a flash of dark to pool in his eyes and the Queen to turn and glare at whoever had yelled.

"Fool," I hissed under my breath.

I may be curious about the boy I had every intention of marrying, but I had been brought up better than to disrespect the King and Queen.

I leaned forward, picking the fool out of the crowd. A Drain thinking they can lift themselves up to a higher stature, no doubt. I would push them out of the way first, send them back to the sewer that they never should have crawled out of.

"Our son is preparing to join many of you at Imdalind Academy and has been working with my nephew, Cail, to prepare. He will be attending school with many of you beginning next week and is excited to meet with you then," Joclyn said, her voice bright even though her eyes were growing dark. Dark as night. Dark as a Drak.

I had heard of the power of a Drak before, the magic focused in sight and prophecy, even though I had never seen it. This time I gasped in shock with all the others.

No one living, besides the Eternals, had seen the Queen give sight. To think that I could see her power...

Before anything else happened, however, the queen's eyes faded back to her signature silver, and she smiled, giving the King a look that ran through the crowd like a wave.

"I dunno about you, Sia," Tasha whispered in my ear. "But maybe you should change your plans to that one," she nodded toward Talon, who was now winking toward a pretty red head near the front. "Then you won't have some sickly Eternal hanging on your arm. The kid hasn't been seen in over a year, Sia. You might be wasting your time."

There was more truth to her words than I wanted to admit, but I didn't give her more than one quick side glance. I had a plan and I was sticking to it. A plan that required me to be first in line for the Gauntlet.

No more fawning over the Eternals, I would be among them soon enough.

"Come on," I growled, hauling Tasha after me as I continued to cut through the crowd. Ilyan had continued his speech, making it easier to navigate through the sea of people who were staring up at him.

"As you know, the Gauntlet began as a way to allow the magic of Imdalind to remain strong in our world. After the Vilỳ were gathered, Joclyn and I built this challenge as a way for all children, from every background and lineage, to hold the power of Imdalind. Children are granted access to this Gauntlet for two years after their seventeenth birthday, and have three chances to successfully complete the race. The first one hundred to pass through the five challenges will be given a kiss from a Vilỳ that will awaken their magic, and are enrolled into Imdalind Academy so they may learn to harness their power.”

“I will be the first,” I said to myself, continuing to haul Tasha after me, aware the girl was still ogling at the platform and the Eternals who were staring down at us like gods and goddesses.

The association was wonderfully accurate.

“On this, the anniversary of the creation of Imdalind Academy, we are pleased to announce that we have worked to make sure that everyone who would like the opportunity to awaken their magic is able to. An additional five hundred interested in seeking their power have been brought here today. We have also worked to give everyone an equal opportunity to join the tradition of the Chosen. We have done this by increasing the student capacity, and will welcome a total of two hundred new Chosen into Imdalind at the end of today. In addition, the challenges have been decreased from five to three and today we will be introducing brand new challenges to our Gauntlet.”

I stopped in place, Tasha slamming into my back as the crowd erupted into a combination of panic, fear, and laughter. Now I knew why there we so many Drains here.

That wasn’t what was heating my blood into a boil, however.

“New quests?”

Outbursts roared through the crowd at his announcement, everyone rushing toward the platform. The Eternals moved to line the edges of the stage. Little Angela had disappeared. All of them stood with hands out, surrounding Ilyan and Joclyn as both their guard and crowd control.

Not that any of us were dumb enough to fight them. They had magic, powerful magic that only the Eternals possessed. Right then we were nothing more than mortals. Mortals that were fighting for their chance to possess even a fraction of what they have.

A chance that had been torn to shreds.

I had been training for those five tasks my entire life. I knew what to do.

Now, I knew nothing.

"We wish you all luck in your endeavor, and will greet the new Chosen once they have awakened from their kiss with magic running through their veins."

Ilyan's final words were drowned out as the screams of anger increased, the low grind of stone and steel echoing over the room as the many doors to the Gauntlet opened.

"Oh my god," Tasha moaned, turning around to face me with wide eyes. "It's starting and we aren't there!"

Everyone raced toward the open door, pushing Tasha and I closer to what should have been our sure thing and compressing us in the mob that my father had warned us about. The mob that could easily destroy our one chance at success.

"Hold on to me, I think I can get us through," Tasha grabbed my wrist as she tried to break me through the crowd, but I pulled away from her touch.

"You're on your own, Tash. If you're lucky, maybe I'll see you on the other side." I gave her a shrug and pushed my way into the crowd, leaving her screeching behind me.

She wasn't my problem anymore.

I didn't even look back as I vaulted over a small girl who had reduced to pathetic tears and pushed passed Miko Christiansen, the first-born son of a Chosen who worked in the King's office. He looked as shocked and bewildered about what had happened, although with one nod it was clear he wasn't going to let it stop him.

There were five hundred more people to fight through the Gauntlet and only two hundred people to get through.

I didn't care what was ahead of me. I would still be the first.

5

GEMMA

"WHO IS READY FOR A PARTY!" EDDY YELLED TO THE LEFT OF ME, the mob of Undermortals that were pressing in on all sides erupting in a scream of excitement and joy. Stark contrasts to the panicked shouts from the Goldens who were still trying to bust their way into the Gauntlet like they were fighting over the first bit of rat.

"Who is ready to sparkle?" The answering yells were accented by fists plunged into the air, screams of war echoing in my ears as the wall of my people raced passed me, throwing themselves into the massive ebony entry that would hold our fate.

Or end.

I would gladly take both. I was ready to face both. Didn't matter how as long as I finished what I came here to do.

"Ready to melt some jewels off their gilded crowns?" I asked to no one in particular, taking one last look at the platform that the royals had stood on a second ago.

The dais was as empty as the massive hall. It was just us and the trash. Literally. The floor was littered with hundreds of those instructions cards, trash, and even a few pools of blood from some altercation as people had tried to get into the Gauntlet first.

Me, Ed, Adrian, Aria, and a few of the others who always tried to plaster themselves to my side would be the last through.

Perfect.

"Let's go, babe," Adrian said, attempting to nuzzle my ear, but I pulled away, leading the last charge through the door and into war.

I was screaming, ready to rip whatever waiting for me into ribbons.

Instead, I was thrust into a suffocating hell.

Air vanished, replaced by a wall of black and ebony that pressed against me until I was sure I could hear my bones crack in my ears. Or I hoped it was bones. I didn't want to think about what the other option was, and if I died from a parlor trick and a cracked skull before I had a chance to light stuff on fire I was going to be really pissed.

Attempting to scream away the pain, I willed myself through the suffocating nothing, screaming and pressing until with a loud pop I fell to the ground. My knees compressed hard against stone, my joints rattling, my lungs burning as they took in air.

Or ash.

Mouthfuls of the stuff were coating my tongue, lining my throat and sending me from heaving to choking as I looked into the flickering light. Into the exploded world that hadn't been here a second ago.

The train station was gone. The high stone walls, and painted murals. Everything and everyone was gone.

I had somehow been transported to a world that was on fire.

Colorful flames licked over buildings and painted the sky like blood dripped in oil. Sparking fire trailed over cobbled roads like snakes, bursting from the sewers and burning through the windows of the fancy homes the Chosen sneered down at us from. It was beautiful the way the opulence burned, the way the pride of our oppressors melted into screams.

It was exactly what I had been dreaming of for years, it was exactly what I had wanted.

Which is why I knew it had to be wrong.

Well, they said they were tests. I wondered what dumb thing I would have to do to prove myself worthy.

"Really?" I scoffed as ten Chosen ripped their way out of the closest burning building, men, women, and children prancing and screaming in contrived fear. "You think this is going to trip me up?"

I rolled my eyes as the poor, defenseless, chosen continued their potty dance and made my way over to them, pulling the large laminated instruction card out of the bag they had given me on check in.

There was also a knife, some rope, and a piece of flint in there. Guess I was going to have to make fire later, too.

"Help us, please!" One of the Chosen screamed in my direction the moment I was within earshot.

Cue the eye roll, I really didn't even need the instructions to know what they wanted me to do here.

Task One: This will test your compassion. Save those with less than yourself in a display of sacrifice and heart.

"Less than yourself?" I scoffed as I looked from the card to the now teary eyed chosen. "Whatever."

I shoved the card back into the bag, and took the last few steps to the Chosen.

"Come with me, scumbags," I snapped, causing all of the Chosen to both jump and cower simultaneously. They looked like a litter of pups we rescued from a testing facility last year. It almost made me forget how terrible they all were.

And then they had to go ahead and open their mouths.

"Fecking Drain," the one closest to me snarled, the girl of no more than ten recoiling against what I was sure was supposed to be her parents.

"Wow. Nice language kid, even I'm not that vulgar." I snapped. I didn't even flinch when the ground rattled with an explosion from a few blocks over. They went back to whimpering and cowering, however. "Come on, let's go."

"Why would we want your help?" The kid's parent continued, while she spit at my feet.

Nice.

"Because otherwise that building is going to collapse on you pretty little face and turn you into a pile of human goo." I smiled wider, while they all flinched at yet another explosion. "That and I am your only option to navigate the sewers. Which is clearly the only safe place left. Take it or take it. I'm not giving you much of a choice."

I pulled out the knife in the bag for effect, causing all of them to scream and cower more. I didn't restrain my laugh that time. They looked freaking ridiculous.

"Come on losers, let's go," I waved the knife toward the open manhole a few feet to the left. They really made this too easy.

The Chosen, however, didn't budge. They cried, cowered, and clung to each other like they had been sewn that way. It wasn't until I brandished the knife a few times and another building off to the left exploded that I was able to herd them.

"Are we your prisoners?" another one of the kids asked, their voice shaking. Poor kid, this apocalyptic war-zone was probably the scariest things they had ever encountered. They wouldn't survive one day underground, and forget about a raid from the CCC. They all would have soiled themselves. Maybe they already did.

"Naw," I scoffed, putting the knife away when we got to the open drain. "I don't keep pets. In you go."

One by one they dropped through the open sewer, still

screaming and crying as the world burned, as the earth rattled as building after building fell to the ground.

"Who knew Chosen were so weak," I laughed to myself as the dark sewer swallowed the last kid, and I jumped after them, ready to get them to the next sanctuary, or whatever was required.

When I touched down, however, they were gone. The darkness had turned to brilliant sun, the sewer now the ruins of a building that looked like the MidCity stop, you know, if it was outside and covered in gold. The place had no roof, although tall stone arches still stretched over the expanse like ribbons. I had seen that in the tunnels before, except I had never seen a sky this blue, seen clouds so white.

It was beautiful. I stood there staring at it, letting the colored sun that streamed through the flowered windows hit against me, it painted me with a sun I didn't know existed.

It was beautiful. Even in ruin, it was beautiful.

I stood. I breathed.

Until a sound I had heard only once before, when a tiny beast had bitten the skin above my elbow, ripped through me. Once was enough, I would never forget that sound. A high-pitched screech of a Vilỳ.

My heart plunged into my gullet, my bones rattled as I shook, as I stared at the pile of rubble that was now starting to shift and heave. As the scream began to multiply.

"Shit." I snapped, grabbing the knife out of the bag. I could easily end the thing with a bit of magic, but it wasn't worth it to use the stuff before the final task. I didn't know if anyone was watching, and I still had bigger plans than picking off a Vilỳ or two.

I held the cold metal thing toward the still shifting rock, toward the bat-like wings and weathered flesh of the monster who poked his head through stone as simply as if he was bursting from hell. Maybe he was, only hell could produce a creature so ugly, with fangs as long as my pinky that dripped with poison, and eyes so red they looked like pools of blood.

"Damn demon bird," I snarled, quickly checking the card to find out how many of these bastards I had to kill and how.

Task Two: This will test your bravery. You must face the world created by the ones who would destroy it. Run from that which you want most to survive, and find the value in fear so as to rebuild the world.

"Run? Yeah, okay. No questions there." Knife in hand, I turned, scanning the ruin for some exit or hiding place. I mean, if you were supposed to run there had to be an exit.

Predictably, there was a door inset into a crumbling wall in the far corner.

"Really? A door?" Gawd, these Eternals had no imagination.

Holding the knife tight in one hand, just in case, I booked it over the piles of rubble and bits of charred wood toward the door as the screech of the Vilỳ was joined by another, and another. The rubble rattled with the sound, the fragments of glass cracking and falling to the floor in splinters of light that reflected against stone so similar to the eyes of the thing that I jumped.

Yes, I fucking jumped. Hearing the gnashing teeth and screaming monsters so close behind me was pulling back every memory of that day. Of what came after. Of the pain.

I hadn't come here for a repeat.

I burst through the door with a yell of my own, turning to slam the thing behind me and lock the beasts away. But once again the damn Gauntlet had other plans and instead of closing the door, I fell face first into stone that smelled like soot and damp. Almost like the musty walls from the old section of the sewers that we don't use anymore because it floods too much, so now the kids go there to hold bonfires and drink stolen hooch.

I think I would have rather been taken there than to wherever this was.

All of the beautiful sunlight was gone. All of the warmth, and the fear, and the screeches of the Vilỳ had been swallowed by an ebony darkness that drowned the world. If it wasn't for the hard stone pressing awkwardly into my cheek, I would have assumed I had been pulled into some kind of underworld.

"Fucking Eternals and their games," I mumbled as I pulled myself up to my hands and knees, shaking my head to expel the low buzzing that was rattling through me.

Buzzing and scraping and mumbled noises that were everywhere. No, not noises, voices.

"Who the fuck is here?" I snapped, now pressing my fingers to my temples to banish the noise.

"Gemma?" I perked up; I would recognize that voice anywhere.

"Ed?"

"Yeah, and Adrian and a few others too," he said with a chuckle that was out of place for the current pitch black nothing we were trapped in. "We all just got here, we were trying to figure out what to do."

"How about we start by getting to the exit," I scoffed, giving the dark nothing that Eddy's voice was buzzing from a wink. Like he could see it. "Oh, this is ridiculous. Where is my bag?"

Somewhere between falling through a door in brilliant sunlight to collapsing on hard stone in utter darkness I had misplaced the bag they had given me. And the knife. And the card. And that little bit of flint that I was sure we were supposed to use to light the card and turn into some kind of a makeshift lamp right about now. As much as I felt around, I wasn't finding much more than stone, however. Cold, damp, stone that wasn't about to light a fire.

Everything else had been pretty obvious, so I was sure this wasn't going to be much different.

"I have a bag," another voice, Adrian, said, from the other side of me.

"Great, get that stone out," I crawled toward where his voice was, feeling my way over the uneven stone and making sure I wasn't about to fall face first into some boulder, or slide into a hole.

"Here ya go, Gemma," Adrian said, making it clear he was holding the stone toward me.

This was worse than when we were all huddled together in the storm cellar during CCC raids. At least then we had to be quiet and weren't hitting people in the face with stones.

Which is exactly what happened.

"Thanks," I huffed with more of a growl, grabbing the stone and striking it against the stone floor hard enough to produce a few sparks. Light blast through the dark like the blast from a bomb, burning my eyes and sparking over the bag and the card that had spilled over the stone beside me.

"Well, that was serendipitous," I laughed, grabbing the card from the ground and reading the last bit in the blinding light the burning card produced. "Task Three: This will test your determination. It will take as much to reach the end."

This one was as dumb and mindless as the others. We just had to get through the dark to the end. This one might actually be hard if they had kept is in the dark to feel our way around like slugs. But instead they give us a light source, instructions, and I'm sure a goal.

I sat up straighter, pushing the extra stone into my pocket and the knife into the bag. I peered through the dark that was threatening to swallow Ed, Adrian, Aria, and the others. They all sat obediently around me, waiting for instructions, all of them looking the same as they had when we had been separated by the suffocating wall. Well, all except Adrian, he had some blood on his shoulder. I wouldn't be surprised if he killed a few Chosen in the first task.

Or all of them.

"So, we have to get through the dark?" Eddy asked as I continued to shift, finally finding a speck of red-tinted light in the distance.

The exit. The end of this dumb test, and where I would make my move. If I had actually been trying to win this thing I would have won in no time.

"Yep, shouldn't be too hard, stay close and I'll get you your magic and through this in one piece," I said, jumping to my feet, moving slowly so as not to extinguish the card.

They all followed suit, well, all except Aria who gave a tiny gasp of surprise that was followed by a snarl, and some prissy Chosen bitch shoved her to the ground. Aria went down, bitch-girl laughed, throwing her sheet of brown hair over her shoulder before she rushed me. Her hand slammed into my chest, sending me stumbling back as she grabbed the stone, knife, and the burning card before bolted into the dark.

"Hey!" Eddy called, his face furrowing in rage before the stolen light began to fade, leaving us all in the dark again.

"Don't worry! They'll get you back to your sewers soon enough!" Her voice carried back to us as she turned, still bolting away, hair sparking in the last of the stolen light before the dark swallowed her.

I really wanted to laugh. The dipshit looked so proud of herself. *Oh yeah, you really put us in our place!*

"Let her go. We don't need that to complete this. The exit isn't far." I rolled my eyes, pulling the other stone back out of my pocket.

"Maybe we will get lucky and take her out too," Adrian said from above me without a hint of a laugh

Yep, he totally killed some Chosen in the first task. I don't know why, but the knowledge made my stomach turn.

"I'm not taking anyone out, Adrian, I'm standing up to them." I gave him a smile he couldn't see and smacked the stone against the floor with a loud clang. My magic sparked at the same time, a few brighter sparks bursting from my fingers to reflect over the stone at the same time.

Thankfully another card was crumpled a step beyond the sparks, all the headstrong Chosen had left the valuable things behind without a thought. They really wouldn't survive a day in our world.

In seconds I had another makeshift torch put together, and lit the other cards until we were standing in an orb of light as bright as the red orb that was looming in the dark, calling to us.

"Okay, that's our destination," I said with a nod to the red light. We need to get as close as we can, then I will send you all through before I end this."

"What are you going to do?" Aria said, the blue in her eyes glinting against the fire that was slowly consuming the instruction cards.

"Make them remember us." I gave her a smile before I turned away, leading them all through the nothing and toward what I was beginning to think was my final destination.

I wasn't ready to give them more of an answer that. Yes, I had promised fireworks, and I was going to give them that. If I said any more I was pretty Adrian would go all hulk protector on me and I would have to zap his balls to get me away from me.

I was here to make a stand, even if that stand was the last one I made. At this point, I was sure I wouldn't come back from this, so I might as well take it as far as I can. Maybe I would get lucky that take out one of the Eternals too.

Just imagining it was a thing of beauty. Thinking of them

begging for forgiveness, me spitting at the feet of the man who had killed so many.

That's what was pulling me forward now. Closer to the end. There was only an abyss between me and finality now, at least I think it was an abyss. It was hard to tell when everything around was a black so dark it appeared to be nothing. Even with five makeshift lamps around us, I was having a hard time making it out.

The massive cavern inside stretched across our path as far as I could see, the gaping hole looking as though someone had broken the ground in half like stale bread. There wasn't any way to jump over the thing, and the flimsy stone bridges that stretched over them were already crumbling, the hollow sounds of stone against stone echoing back up to us as pieces fell off and tumbled their way down to whatever hell awaited them below.

Of course, that might have been the people that were blindly running toward the exit and stumbled into the gaping hole. Swallowed by the earth.

My heart was in my chest as I led us forward, giving everyone one silent look as we reached the bridge that looked to be the least likely to send us to our deaths.

"Stay close, but move quick," I hissed behind me, before I bolted over the thing, making the trek first. I wasn't about to make any of my people test the thing. Besides, if it collapsed, I was sure I could figure out how to magic my way back up. Or explode things on my way down.

Either way.

"Eddy, you come last," I instructed as I took my last step, a jagged piece of stone falling from the bridge. The sound of collapsing stone grated against my already ragged nerves. We needed to hurry.

With each step, more rock fell away. By the time we got to Ed there would be nothing left. Hand after hand, I helped everyone else to stable footing as Eddy helped them on to the narrow thing across from me.

So close.

Only Eddy and Aria were left, my hand reaching out to the girl when a rock hurled through the air, zipping right behind Aria before hitting Ed right in the head. With an agonizing howl, he went down, grabbing at the stone in an attempt to keep himself up.

"Gawd!" I yelled, pushing Adrian away as I tried to figure out a way to pull him up. Just like moving the man hold cover, there had to be a way.

Aria turned, reaching down to help Eddy up, just as a second stone hit her shoulder. Her quick movement had put her off balance, and the stone was like the last stick on a dwindling fire.

I watched in slow motion as Aria lost her footing and began to fall, arms outstretched, fingers searching for the hands that were seconds to slow to catch her. I was on my knees, clinging to stone as I reached over the edge, as Eddy turned and stretched, but we grabbed nothing but the air that was warm and swirling as my magic flared, unable to do more than slow her down.

It wasn't enough.

"Aria!" I yelled, her name echoing over stone as her own scream swallowed my agony. As the dark swallowed her. As everything slowed down, as the world turned red.

"She's fine. She belongs down there anyway."

I tensed, my spine stiffening as though it had been zipped up. Every muscle, every bone, every boiling nerve ending was ready to attack the girl who stood on the other side of the bridge, smiling at me, bouncing a rock in her hand.

My anger boiled at the smug smile she gave us, the disgusted twist in her lip deepening as she jumped, using Eddy's face as a launchpad to land right before me. Right in my line of fire.

Inches from her death.

It wouldn't take much.

It wouldn't take anything more than a finger pressed against her heart. But using my magic on her would eliminate my ability to rise against the Eternals.

Against her.

"You all do, you should give up now, there is no place for you in our world." She flipped her hair in my face before turning toward the red light, ready to run into the massive opening and the figures that were just beyond.

Toward the end.

Perfect timing.

"Where the hell do you think you're going? No one hurts my people and gets away with it." I snatched her arm before she could take more than a few steps, pulling her back with a tug that should have sent her down into the abyss after Aria, but she held her ground.

As if that would help her.

"Get your hands off of me, Drain, or I'll make sure the next time the CCC liberates a sewer they track you down as a special favor. My mother would see to it. We could use a new toiletry maid." She yanked her arm out of my grasp, the shock at what she had said sinking in. The CCC. She knew them.

She was them.

I should have recognized her at once. She had her mother's eyes, the woman who screamed at her Tarn army, who pushed them to murder us, who spoke for the king. His puppet, and our executioner.

Samantha Demarco. I didn't even know what her spawns name was, but I didn't care. She deserved what was coming for her.

"See you soon." She waved and took off, and I let her go. Let the red light of the ending frame her like the target in a bullseye.

"What are you doing Gemma? Don't let her get away!"

Adrian snapped, his hand pushing against my back and shoving me toward the girl. God, that guy needed to get a grip.

"Shut up Adrian," I snapped, pushing him back with as much force. Okay, maybe a little more. "Remember who you're talking to. I'm going to make sure she is right where I want her before we finish what we came here to do. She will be the first to burn."

My magic was raging through me with more anger and fury than I had ever felt. It buzzed in my veins. It raged through my fingers.

She turned, the sneer dropping from her lips as she saw me, saw the violet magic. Magic the same shade as my eyes rippled over my skin, it licked the ground around me. The spectacle reflected in her eyes, the wide horrified orbs showing a power that I didn't think I held.

It would be my perfect last act.

For all the people they all killed. For all the people they had taken. For my mother, for my father. For Aria.

For freedom.

They would remember us now. They would never forget.

"All the glitters were never gold."

6

———

ROWAN

BLACK WAS EVERYWHERE, THE ROOM OF THE LAST CHALLENGE OF the Gauntlet nothing more than shades of grey against an ebony world. Those who were running the Gauntlet had to simply get from the open door behind them to the speck of light before them, where the Skříteks, my father's people and the guards who live with and protect the 'royal family', were waiting to administer the bite of the Vilỳ to the first two hundred runners. There were pitfalls and obstacles in between, of course, but all of them were concealed by the dark.

Dark to test your determination or some such shit. My parents had done something similar to me years before.

I wouldn't have recognized it if it wasn't for that, if my father hadn't proudly given me a tour of his creation just days before, if I hadn't recognized the depth of his magic as he created the space.

If I hadn't realized that my dreams were no longer dreams at all.

Damn it. I was trapped in a sight. No, not a sight. I refused to think of it like that. A premonition.

My mind was trapped in the black with everyone else,

surrounded by heaves of exertion, gasps of shock, and the panicked threats of the runners. The noise echoed around me as everyone tried to make their way through.

Great. The one place I had no interest in being, and I got stuck here anyway.

"Get your hand off of me, Drain, or I'll make sure that the next time the CCC liberates a sewer they track you down as a special favor. My mother would see to it. We could use a new toiletry maid." The unfamiliar girl's snap was so full of acid and hatred that I could feel it twist against my spine as if the emotion was my own.

My head swam with it, the vision shimmering as two indiscernible figures pulled out of the dark and into shadow. Two girls. One, a beauty with chestnut brown hair that fell to her waist, was walking away from the other, taking the light with her and leaving them in shadow.

"What are you doing Gemma? Don't let her get away!" Some guy snapped, his voice a bark in the smothering dark. Whatever light these people had been hovering around had gone, I couldn't even see shadows now.

"Shut up Adrian. I'm letting her get closer before we finish what we came here to do." A familiar voice snarled just as a spark pulled through the ebony nothing. Violet magic swallowed the dark, a spark of power dripping from bare fingers, revealing a scarred hand, a tattooed arm and that smug smile I had seen hundreds of times before.

The girl. The girl from my dreams, from my sight. She had magic. Illegal, damaged, uncentered magic. The Undermortals weren't using a bomb, she had been bitten by a Vilỳ. We hadn't caught them all as we had thought.

All of those attacks, the reason that girl had been haunting my dreams.

It was all leading up to this. A rebellion. A dangerous fight that had the potential to hurt hundreds.

That I needed to stop.

I didn't even have time to be pissed that my Drak power was good for something. I needed to get out of this damn dream, out of this sight and warn them.

"She will be the first to know what we can do."

Screams echoed through the dark as the violet blast exploded from her hand. Flames devoured everything; the dark, the stone, even the screams as the illegal magic turned back to the red that normally followed a sight.

"No! Stop!" I was up and heaving, hand reaching forward as my mind replayed the explosion. As I tried to stop it.

Stop it.

I needed to stop it.

I tried to untangle myself from my bedding, but cotton sheets knotted around my feet as my thick comforter wound round my knees. My panicked attempt to reach my desk and my phone turned me into a large cotton boulder and down I went.

With a hollow thud, I landed on a pile of dirty shirts and underwear and apparently my TV remote, because the thing snapped on to the worst thing possible: the live feed from the Gauntlet.

My parents stood on the raised platform, Uncle Ryland and Aunt Wyn on either side, all of them staring over the mass of people that clogged the former train station.

Great, it hadn't started yet. I still had time.

"Quiet please." My father's booming voice rattled the old speakers on the television set, bouncing over the stone walls of my underground bedroom as the camera zoomed in on the massive platform.

Thank god most of my aunts, uncles, and cousins were with them. Perhaps my mom had already seen something.

"We will begin the challenge in a few minutes." I didn't think my dad ever really turned the king off, but right then he was all King Ilyan. His back was an iron rod, his blue eyes narrowed at the crowd in such a way that I was sure he had used his magic on them all to get them to shut the hell up.

I've been on the receiving end of that a few times. Glad he was behind the screen this time.

"Okay dad, tell them all about your big plan," I mumbled to myself as I wiggled my way out of the mess of sheets and blankets and back toward the mess on my desk that was concealing my phone. This was going to be cutting it close.

"I, and my family, are proud to join you for this, the seventieth anniversary of this competition. We are proud of the Chosen that have wielded the magic of Imdalind since we first began this challenge, and are eager to welcome more into Imdalind at the completion of this race."

"Where's Rowan?" The muffled interruption was barely audible through the television set, but it might as well have slapped me anyway. I turned to the static image as it panned from my father to the hundreds of eager faces.

The crowd was massive, full of more Undermortals than I had seen in one place, and more of the Chosen's children than had run in years past. I didn't need the question from the crowd to know that Talon's prediction from weeks before had been correct. I was supposed to be starting at the Academy this year, and they were all there because of me.

Well, not me specifically, but an Eternal, *any* Eternal, at the school. I was sure some of them had waited to run the Gauntlet just to be in my year.

Sick.

"Our son is preparing to join many of you at Imdalind Academy and has been working with my nephew, Cail, to prepare." You had to hand it to my mom, she was strangely good at lying. "He will be attending school with many of you beginning next week and is excited to meet with you then."

Really good at lying. Or being diplomatic. I wasn't sure what the difference was.

Her voice faded off, the tone growing hollow as her silver eyes dimmed. I knew that look. And not because the tiny strands of hair on the back of my neck were lifting up, my focus drifting in and out as sight had tried to connect me with her. I had simply seen it enough in her.

I turned back to my desk, pushing away the Drak magic that was trying to connect us, but not before one flash of sight was able to wiggle its way through.

It wasn't the blast I had seen, however, nor the explosion, or the girl with the mohawk, but just an angry crowd, covered with dirt. She didn't know.

"Shit."

The King and Queen exchanged a look that the crowd had no chance to interpret, but Talon and Dramin had seen, and Patrice was already shuffling my little sister off the makeshift dais.

"Double shit." Back to the phone.

"As you know, the Gauntlet was begun as a way to allow the magic of Imdalind to remain strong in our world. After the last Vilỳ was gathered, Joclyn and I built this challenge as a way for all children, from every background and lineage to hold the power of Imdalind. Children are granted access to this Gauntlet for two years after their seventeenth birthday and have three chances to successfully complete the race. The first one hundred to pass through the five challenges will be given a kiss from a Vilỳ that will awaken their magic and are enrolled into Imdalind Academy so as to harness their power."

Notes from Angie, half eaten bagels, an old record my aunt Wyn had sent me last month. Everything was on my desk but the damn phone. My blood was boiling, fear and frustration rolling through my veins as my magic picked up in one boiling wave. I didn't have time for this! I smacked my palms flat on the desk, my magic surging through the wood, through the air and buoying every single object above the desk. Papers, records, and half eaten bits of food hovered a foot above the worn wood surface, the cell phone spinning like a top in the middle of them.

"Finally." I snapped the phone out of the air, letting everything collapse back to the desk with a clatter as my dad's roaring voice continued in the background.

"On this, the anniversary of the creation of Imdalind Academy, we are pleased to announce that we have worked to make sure everyone who would like the opportunity to awaken their magic is able to. An additional five hundred who are interested in seeking their power have been brought here today. We have also worked to give everyone an equal opportunity to join the tradition of the Chosen, by increasing the students we will welcome into Imdalind to two hundred and introducing brand new challenges to our Gauntlet."

I was only half way through the text when the screams ripped through the television, rattling the old speakers as fear and anger ripped through the crowd. Ripped through me.

Angie was gone, all of my aunts and uncles and cousins having taken her place as they stood around the King and the Queen. I guess it's good I hadn't gone. I would have been shuffled away like Angie. Even at eighteen, I was not considered nearly old enough to be an adult in my family.

My family.

All of which appeared to be there, which meant I was the only one left in the caves of Imdalind. Good for them to stop whatever was about to happen. Bad for me.

"We wish you all luck in your endeavor, and will greet the

new Chosen once they have awakened from their kiss with magic running in their veins." my dad yelled over the angry shouts as they all backed off the stage, the camera panning over the crowd as they flooded toward the double doors that had been thrown open. The crowd had turned into a mob.

The children of the Chosen were climbing over each other to be the first through. But they were the only ones that had ridden their fancy panties up their ass. All of the Undermortals had clustered near the back of the crowd, walking slowly toward the opening as they laughed, yelled, and nodded toward the girl that was in the center of the group, her bright pink mohawk lifting a foot above everyone else.

"Well, holy fuck on a chipped china plate."

I really shouldn't have been surprised, and I was more pissed than surprised. Damn Drak magic and all that.

Screw the text.

Pressing my thumb against the phone, I let my magic surge into it, buzzing the thing to life and connecting me right to the one person who would understand and probably not flip her shit about all of this.

"Hello?" Her little voice buzzed through the phone's speaker, mixing with the announcer as the last of the Undermortals vanished through the Gauntlet doors, the massive things snapping shut behind them.

"Angie, it's Rowan. I need you to do something for me."

"Row? What's going on? Everything here is scary all of a sudden." I cringed, I could hear the shake in her voice, the sound eating me up. I was about to make that scary a whole lot worse.

"Yeah, Angie, it's important. I need you to tell mom that you saw an explosion, in the black room. Tell her there is a bomb."

It wasn't quite the truth and it twisted in my gut. I knew what I had seen, that girl had magic. They needed to know, they needed to stop her, and I stood thousands of miles away, watching an empty train station on the television, lying to my sister. Protecting the last person on earth that I should be.

"Rowan," She hissed into the phone, her voice muffled as she held the receiver too close. She may be just a kid, but Angie was nowhere near dumb, or gullible. "Did you see something?"

"No."

She scoffed at my lie; the look she was giving me clear in my mind's eye. We had played this game a few times, hopefully she wouldn't put up too much of a fight. I couldn't glare back at her and threaten to take away her extra dessert this time.

"I need you to do this Angie," I may have been pleading to an eight-year-old, but luckily this eight-year-old understood.

"An explosion in the black room," she repeated, and the knot in my chest loosened, although not enough. My magic was still on a rampage, the dizziness pulling at my neck again.

I wished it would fuck off, but I knew what it was trying to tell me. I was clearly going off the deep end if I was starting to think my magic was talking to me.

I might already be drowning given that I was listening.

"Yeah, tell her you think it's magic." I cringed. I couldn't keep it away from her, but saying it aloud felt like a betrayal.

"Okay, Row," she whispered, the sound of voices in the background picking up as talk of rebellions and a robbery filtered through the phone in muffled static.

"Be safe, Angie," I whispered as she called out to mom, Talon's laugh nearly drowning her out.

"Mom, I think I saw something..."

Everything loosened, my magic settling as I collapsed back down to my bed, the mattress sagging beneath me, calling for me to just lay back and go back to sleep. I would love nothing more, but I couldn't tear myself away from the TV, not yet, not before I knew that they had stopped it. That everyone was safe.

"What are you talking about," my mom's voice broke through the phone's speaker, all muffled and crackled as she stepped closer to Angie. "Who is on the phone Angela?"

Shit. Full name.

So much for that plan.

I had expected her to snatch the phone and demand answers. Instead, my room was filled with the smell of sulfur as a loud bang rattled the crap on my dresser, and my mother stood right before me looking furious as the golden ribbon swirled around her.

"Spill."

"I saw the girl..."

"What girl?" She snapped before I could continue, her eyes flashing from black to silver in a haunting firework as she tried to see what I had seen. The increasing furrow in her brow made it clear that she could not.

"I've been dreaming of a girl."

"You've been having sight? This whole time?" Her whole expression changed, from worry to something more like awe. No, pride. Ugh.

"No mom, dreams. I've been having dreams of the girl who's been exploding the shops." My words caught in my throat, a heavy weight pressing against my throat. It was so much more than a few acts of rebellion. I had seen her whole life. But I wasn't about to get into that.

"I just saw her, in the last cave."

"How long have you been seeing her?"

"That doesn't matter, Mom! There's going to be an attack, we have to get back there..."

Any further explanation was swallowed by a static scream that echoed through the television. The image shifted, everything shaking as pieces of the ancient ceiling of the train station collapsed to the ground, as a lavender blast broke through the ancient doors and swallowed everything.

We stood, staring at television static as my own screams echoed in my ears.

"No," I whispered, "We're too late."

"What in the world?" She gasped, hand flying to her mouth in shock. "How did I miss this...?"

"She has magic, Mom. The girl. She was bitten by a Vilỳ." My heart ached, my soul twisting as I stepped toward the TV. As if me being there would help what had happened.

No, so I could protect her.

"You are going to explain everything later." My mother heaved, turning to me and giving me a look I could not place before she snatched my hand and pulled me into the void of color and energy that she had arrived there in. I had always been told only Draks and those with very strong magic could accomplish a stutter, could move between space like some old TV show. I had seen my parents do it multiple times, perhaps I had even longed for it.

I would never long for it again.

Twisting, burning, suffocating. My skull might have been trying to turn itself inside-out if only to fit through the straw I was being stuffed through better.

Thankfully it ended, although it left me gasping on my hands and knees, staring at the black charcoal floor of the room they had created as a final task.

Although it wasn't as I had just seen it days before, or even minutes ago. The magic was gone, the lights were turned on, and everything was full of blood, panic, and agony.

Everything except for the girl who kneeled ahead of us, a smug smile on her face as she looked up at my father, her hands bound and tied by my Aunt Wyn's fire magic. She wasn't going anywhere.

"What accomplices do you have here?" I had never heard my father sound so angry, so powerful, before.

I tried to take a step back, but my mother held onto me tighter, dragging me forward. Closer.

The rage in my parent's voices was shivering through me in a wave that begged me to flee. She, however, was still, chin up, not a drop of fear in her eyes as she faced his scorn.

"All the glitters were never gold," she snarled, spitting at his feet with a glob of bright red spit, the color perfectly matching the bloody smile she gave him.

The grin was not returned.

One thing was, however, but not from my father, from my brother.

"Talon stop!" I yelled, pulling the girls focus, eyes that appeared to be almost purple digging into me for the first time and freezing any warning in place. It wouldn't have mattered anyway, Talon's fist had intersected with her temple, sending her to the floor.

7

————

GEMMA

"HEY GUYS, SHE'S AWAKE. I WOULD GET YOUR ASSES DOWN HERE before I boil them."

I wasn't sure what constituted as awake to whoever had spoken, but this sure wasn't it. Whatever that douche prince had hit me with felt like it might have left a giant hollow in the side of my skull. Maybe his hands were made of rock. My ears were ringing, the light above my head sparking in a starburst of knives grinding against my skull. Every joint throbbed as though they had come alive, my fish-limped body flopped over the hard ridges of a cold metal chair.

I wasn't even sure how he could tell I was awake.

I was used to being achy and sore after using my magic, but this felt more like near death torture. Still, I had experienced worse. I wasn't about to let it stop me from breaking out of here.

I had accomplished half of my task; the Gauntlet was blown to ribbons. The king and queen had to be close by, I could still finish this.

I could still fight for my people. Give all those who had passed the Gauntlet before my blast something to fight for. Lay the way for them to change our world.

I shifted in my seat, ready to break out of this prison and murder some royals, but an electrical firestorm ran up my arms and down my spine with the tiny motion. So much for knives grinding against my skull. Everything exploded, white popping in my vision as I arched and contorted, fighting back a scream before I collapsed against the folding chair that I had been tied to.

Magical binding from hell and a scratchy rope around my wrists.

I couldn't be offended that they hadn't restrained me with more, or killed me on the spot, if only because it proved just how stupid the Eternals were.

I was going to pick them off like rats in the drain.

I spit the bitter blood that filled my mouth at the bright red shoes of whoever was pacing in front of me, landing the glob against a cracked tile floor before his toe.

"All the glitters were never gold," I drawled, my words slung together as the ache in my jaw grew.

"Yes, so you've said." The same voice from before spoke with a bored drawl, his words slurred, but I had a feeling that was more from my brain having been electrocuted. Or the exhaustion from exploding a whole cave.

Shaking, I lifted my head, narrowing my eyes at the guy in the middle of the room. He stood like he thought himself to be much cooler than he really was; his arms were folded over a leather jacket, dreads pulled back into a weird low braid, blue eyes narrowed right at me.

"Thomas." The word dripped with more than my blood.

The King's brother. I glared at him, mentally flicking through all of the information we had gathered on him over the years.

Born a thousand years ago, sometime in the 1200s in France. Thomas, or Thom as he was known to the royals, was married to

Wynifred who was the most famous of the Trpaslíks. Trpaslíks: rock magic, manipulation of earth. Thom was the son of the old mad king and a once mortal princess.

They had two children, although a bit of surveillance picked up by one of the Undermortals last year said that there might be three, not that it mattered. Cail and Analine were the important ones, they ran Imdalind Academy.

"The king's brother."

"Yes, and what is your name?"

"I would rather die nameless, taking you down in the name of my people." I had meant it as a threat, but my words were still slurred. He smiled at me, one guffaw of a laugh shaking his shoulders.

"I'm sure you would." He pulled a chair around to face me, the metal grinding against the old tile floor with a sound that mixed painfully with the high-pitched shrieking that was still rattling my ears.

I refused to cringe, I just glared, searching for clues about where I was. The walls were bare grey blocks, the edges crumbling into little piles of sand on the ground. Any paint that had been there was long gone. There was no table, no windows, nothing but the two chairs we sat in and an old wood door, the golden knob covered with blood.

The room could have been one of the annex rooms that we sometimes found in the tunnels, which given the blood told me exactly where we were.

"We are still in the Gauntlet. You still cleaning up that mess I made?" I smiled, letting my blood coated teeth flash.

"We are in the station outside of Berlin," Thom corrected, not that any of that made sense to me. I hadn't known where the vans were going to take us, and I haven't paid attention to any of the announcements seeing as I hadn't planned on coming back.

Blow up the damn race. Blow up the King and Queen, and

get our message out. I was halfway there.

"And why are you the one guarding me? Was there no one stronger?" I asked, spitting another glob of blood, my mouth still filling with the bitter stuff. I narrowly missed his shoes that time and he shifted them beneath his chair.

"Strength is not an issue. I'm the only one who wouldn't lose my cool and kill you on sight." He didn't even smile. I had a feeling that he was serious. Wimp. Made getting out of here easier.

"I guess I should be flattered." I was never one to put on the charm, and it worked about as well as it always did. Meaning it didn't. Thom snorted until his nostrils flared.

"Flattery must mean something drastically different nowadays."

"Only that you have severely underestimated me." I gave him a wink, pointing my toes as I prepared to shift forward and break the chair and the flimsy rope around my wrists. My magic was ready, I was ready. It was time to get out of here. I didn't move more than an inch against the rope before the same fire flared through my bones.

One tiny scream escaped as my back arched, pain snapping the bones together before I was slammed back in the chair, teeth ground together, as I forced my head from its contortion to stare at the man as I heaved.

"I wouldn't do that if I were you. I might be *weak*," he rolled his eyes, "but it's my wife's magic that's holding you, and she is ruthless. Her magic is made to kill after all, so I wouldn't fight too much."

That I didn't know. We had found nearly nothing out about Wynifred in our years of spying, research, and espionage.

"If she's so ruthless why didn't she kill me the second I dropped the ceiling on the would-be-murderer?" I snarled, leaning forward and receiving another zap.

That time I did little more than grit my teeth together. So much for being made to kill, a few more of those and I was sure I could power my way past it, reignite my magic, and get back to wreaking havoc.

"Maybe she will. Before that, the king and queen wish to speak to you," he said, leaning back in his chair.

I could have pissed myself. How bat-shit stupid were these Eternals? Before I could ask, the door behind Thom swung open, the tiny room filling with people.

Skřítek guards poured in first, hands out in preparation for attack. I didn't see a drop of magic, but I could feel it. It weighed against the air, pressing against my chest like a soaked blanket after a flood.

I had never felt anything like it. I had always been the only one with magic, but with so many around me, I could feel it.

I could taste it.

The guard was immediately followed by the king's other brother, Ryland and his wife Mira. The two changed places with Thom who slipped out with only a few words in a language I didn't understand, holding the door open for the King and Queen.

Those two glared into me with an intensity I hadn't seen since my mother died, scorn and disappointment mixed with a tiny bit of what was that... surprise?

Awe?

Seriously?

What was wrong with these people? Showing me awe after I ripped their precious Gauntlet to shreds? I was totally laughing, the sound confusing the guards who were looking between me and the queen like she had some alarm system. Oh yeah, the whole seeing the future thing.

She would have to prove that before I would believe it.

"Your Majesties," I snarled, pushing mockery into each word

as I bowed my head, fighting against the restraints and the magic that was trying to melt my bones.

I didn't so much as flinch that time, it still hurt, but I wasn't about to let them know. Seeing those two before me was turning my magic into a cyclone. The energy buzzed through my veins, pressing against my fingers in need of attack.

I pushed it back. I wouldn't be able to even get to the King and Queen if I attacked right now, and with how my magic drained me I only had one shot.

Patience.

"We have been waiting quite a while for you to wake up," Queen Joclyn said, her voice soft as she stepped forward.

I scoffed, leaning back on the chair and getting another soft zap.

"You wouldn't have had to wait so long if your meathead of a son hadn't knocked me out."

She didn't smile, she just stepped closer to me, past all the people I had assumed had been there to guard her. None of them moved in, even though I was at reaching distance now.

"Yes, well, my darling *meathead* seemed to think you were a danger to those around you. I'm still not convinced that you are."

"I just blew up your precious Gauntlet, hopefully killed that bitch that was shoving all of us *Drains* off that cliff, too. Maybe even a few more. And you still aren't convinced I'm a danger? You are as dumb as a sack of rat bones, lady."

I spat blood at her feet, a few guards shuffling their feet closer. Still, no magic dripped from them, even though the pressure of it in the air was growing.

None of the Eternals reacted, they just stared at me. The Queen took another step closer, her eyes narrowed until I was sure she could see right through me. They weren't as silver anymore.

They were dark, like clouded iron, or the sky through the grate on a rainy day.

If I hadn't been tied to the chair, I probably would have fallen right out of it. That look was creepy as hell.

I shifted my weight, sparking another fiery assault on my nerve endings and leaned closer instead.

"We have seen worse in an untrained child," Joclyn said, thankfully looking away and giving me a chance to breathe. "I don't believe that anyone is past saving anymore."

For some reason, Ryland and his wife were snickering in the corner. It was only adding to the nervous edge that was twisting up my spine.

"Well, get ready for the ultimate regret."

"There is very little I regret, Gemma." That sent me right back in my chair.

"Take it you've been speaking to my people, seeing as you know my name."

"We have been speaking to your colleagues, yes." King Ilyan said from the back of the room, stepping around his brother to face me. "Eddy, Adrian, the little girl, Aria…"

I jumped forward in my chair, earning myself another zap. "Aria. She's alright?"

I knew in that moment I had given myself away. Too much emotion, my one weakness cracking through and breaking the Queen's voice into a smile.

"See, no one is too far into evil." King Ilyan stepped back, turning to the guards and prattling on in that same weird language Thom had spoken in. The guards smacked their heels against the floor and rushed away, leaving me alone with the Eternals.

Alone. With. The. Eternals.

Morons.

"Now, I would like to know about your magic."

"What do you want to know? I got bit by one of your little flying devil birds, I slept and when I woke up you had taken away everything that mattered. Pretty straight forward. Pretty standard story for when you build yourself a villain." I gave them a wide smile, letting another zap of fire move through my veins as I leaned forward.

The magic no longer hurt, and it wasn't numbing my own power quite as much anymore. I was getting closer.

"We were clearly wrong about having caught all the Vilÿ's, and for that I am sorry," Queen Joclyn said, sitting in the chair that Thom had vacated, looking strangely human as she sat flanked by the two brothers.

Human. She was born as one. Well, she was raised as one. She was always magic, and after Ilyan *saved* her from something that the history books were never quite clear about she and Ilyan saved us all in the war two hundred years ago.

It was all common knowledge. We hadn't even researched her; everyone knew her story. Who knew how true it was or how much she had betrayed us? She was like us, but she had forgotten us.

"Sorry? Don't be sorry. It gave me the power to care for my people. To end this monarchy and defeat you all." I said, giving her a twisted smile. "But I have a feeling you already know all of that."

The threat was clear, yet the King's dumb brother Ryland chuckled. Mira gave him a look as she walked around the group, giving herself a better line of sight to my hands, the queen, and the door. She might have had the most sense of them all.

"A bit. We've been watching you for months, Gemma." I really hated the way she said my name. "Grocery stores. Banks. Clothing stores. I'm impressed. Most of the Chosen can do little more than make pencils explode in their first month--"

"Flattery is not going to work on me, lady. Of course, I can do more than your damn Chosen. I wasn't bit last month, I worked for almost nine years to get this strong. All with one goal." I was looking right at her now, my magic rampaging through my veins.

"Yes, so you've said," King Ilyan barked, stepping behind the Queen like some kind of gigantic reverse bodyguard.

Mira stood behind me, and the king behind Joclyn, it was getting harder and harder to make my shot count.

"We are aware of the class discrepancy, and are already taking steps to change it---"

"Class discrepancy?" I cut him off, laughing like a loon. "You bring your Chosen armies into our homes. You kill our people, you force us into slavery, and you call it a class discrepancy?"

Silence bathed the room, the four powerful giants glancing between themselves with looks that ranged from horror, to confusion.

"Don't stand there pretending you haven't done this. I've watched hundreds dragged off by that Tarn army of yours. Watched the CCC shackle children and put them to work in the glimmering homes of your Chosen, in the radioactive mines." I snarled, twisting my hands against the ropes as Mira finally stepped around to face me, all of them staring down at me in what was clearly shock.

"Oh my god. You didn't know," I gasped, leaning forward as I put some counter pressure against the ropes. "Some leaders you are. My people are being slaughtered and you had no clue. You deserve what's coming to you."

I would have attacked there, I was ready, my hand was almost free and their dumb faces would have given them the most perfect end. But then that damn queen had to open her mouth and sweeten the deal.

"I wonder if you might give us a few minutes." It was like

fucking Christmas. But with actual presents and not just an extra rat on the spit.

I didn't hide my glee as I smiled at her, her eyes narrowing as everyone else left without so much as an argument.

It was her and me now.

My hand slipped out of the rope, quickly followed by the other. I barely caught the heavy coils before they fell to the ground, the thick cords twisted around my fingers as I held my hands behind my back. Free. Ready.

"I sure hope you don't regret this." She would. She really, really would.

"I don't regret much," Joclyn said again, straightening her ridiculous skirt, the former beige covered with the reds and browns of destruction. "But I do regret what has happened to your people."

God, I could have shit a brick. This woman sure had an ego on her if she thought all of this was going to be that easy.

"You think a dumb apology is going to fix this? You are way past that. Stop pacifying me lady," I snarled, letting my magic flare, the sparks dripping onto the rope and singeing it. Everything was in working order.

"I am not trying to pacify you." Stubborn and ego. No wonder this whole place was gone to shit if this was who was leading us.

"Lying won't work either." The air was starting to smell now, my magic building into full strength as I infected the rope with my magic, turning it into a bomb.

"Did you know I started the school specifically to stop this kind of thing from happening?" She took a step closer to me, the same weight I had felt before pressing against my chest, like her magic was trying to hold me down all on its own.

"Didn't do a very good job then, did you?"

"No, I didn't."

"Excuse me?" My heart stuttered as I dropped the rope to the floor, knowing that it could explode any second. Suddenly I didn't want it to.

"I failed you all. Of course, with everything that has been happening being done in secret--"

"So much for your super 'I can see the future' party trick," I snapped as the rope exploded.

Screaming, I jumped up, sending every bit of magic I had right toward her.

Sparks of red and purple filled the room, my chair slamming to the floor before the rope exploded again, sending the twisted metal and a good amount of rock into the air.

I watched her, ready to see her fall to the ground, to see fear in her face. I was ready for it, ready for the door to slam open and the King to kill me. For everything to be over. To have won.

But the Queen just smiled, blinking once as everything froze, rubble and smoke held in place, bits of rock dangling in the air before the magic I had sent her way reversed. My attack hit against me, slamming into my chest and sending me soaring through the tiny room and into the hard-stone wall behind me.

The door never opened. It was still her and I in an empty room, me plastered against a crumbling wall as everything around me started to move in reverse, smoke swirling into nonexistence, rope un-burning, the chair putting itself back together.

"You are strong, Gemma, I will give you that," Joclyn said, walking calmly toward me, her magic holding me against the wall, feet dangling a good foot above the ground that had begun putting itself back together.

One swipe of her hand and the room looked exactly as it had seconds before. Well, all except the sacrificial lamb that was pinned to the wall.

What the hell?

The Queen was standing inches from me. She wasn't flinching. Her hand wasn't moving. There wasn't a whisper of her magic in the room save the pressure on my chest, and yet everything I had done was gone. We had assumed her weak, we had assumed her easy to defeat.

We were so fucking wrong.

I wanted to piss my pants and run away, instead I tightened my jaw and glared down at her. Down because she was still holding me against the wall.

"You have more strength than most of the Chosen I have seen. I'm impressed."

"Don't be impressed. Don't be anything but dead. I want nothing from you. I'm nothing like you!" Fighting against her was doing next to nothing, but I still gave it my all, wiggling as I roared.

"That's where you are wrong. Whether you like to admit it or not, we agree on one very important point."

"And what is that?" I tried to snarl, but between the pressure of her magic against my chest and wasting the last of my energy on a useless attack, all I managed was little more than a gasp.

"That this is more than a class discrepancy. We didn't know it, but if what you said is true, and I assume it is, then you are right. You are both right. This is approaching a dangerous war that could end the lives of thousands, and it needs to end."

I stopped fighting against her, the last of my strength swallowed in the shock of what she said.

"We didn't invite all of the mortals to the Gauntlet to laugh at them, Gemma. We want this to change. Magic should not just be for the few. It appears my attempt to make it equal has only ended in disaster," Joclyn continued, her magic releasing and letting me slide to the floor.

Too bad I didn't have the strength to hold myself up. My legs crumpled, sending me to the ground in some weird pretzel shape.

"And you didn't see this coming?" I scoffed at her, pushing myself against the wall in an attempt to stay upright, to face her head on and not like some worm I was sure she saw me as. Queen or not I wasn't interested in groveling underneath her.

"Sight is an interesting thing. It is powerful and varied but not exact. It can show everything, or it can show nothing. It can also be blocked by things more powerful than you give them credit for."

"Ha! After what you just did? What in the world could be more powerful than you?" I tried to laugh, but I was truly terrified of that possibility. She had put a room back together with a blink, stopped my attack, and a hair wasn't out of place. It was frightening to think something could be more powerful than that.

"I think I will leave that mystery for you to unravel." She smiled and pulled the repaired chair toward us, but she didn't sit, she just held out her hand to me.

"You really have a death wish, don't you?"

"No. You're too weak to do anything and I know how uncomfortable floors can be."

Weak? Maybe, but that didn't mean I was going to give into her Royal Highness.

"I'm fine thanks." My snarl didn't quite translate.

What the hell was up with this lady? I mean, she was right. Even if I had the strength, I wasn't about to try to attack her again. But wasn't I supposed to be her prisoner or something?

"I want to make you a proposition, Gemma," she said, taking the seat that she had pulled around for me. "We need people like you in this world, people with strength and courage and a moral compass that doesn't point toward utter destruction."

"You did notice that I exploded your Gauntlet, right?"

She smiled, "And I am not one to believe that all actions are rooted in a nefarious cause."

"You sound like my mom." Even after so long, thinking of her still hurt. It was an ache of weakness, however, and I pushed it away.

No room for that nonsense.

"Well, I do have a son about your age, so let's say I am practiced in giving talks like this." She smiled like she was telling a joke.

I stared at her. "What is this proposition?"

"I would like you to attend Imdalind Academy along with one of your friends from the Gauntlet. Many other mortals won the Gauntlet and will be joining you, but you and one other will both be granted special enrollment. In addition, the friend you choose will be given a bite from one of the Vilỳ from my home."

"You want to take me, and a friend, into your school and you don't think I will just blow up the joint?"

"Well, your magic will be restrained until you can prove an increase in skill and compassion."

Compassion? I was not the one who needed to learn compassion. I had been keeping the people that were dying right under her nose alive.

"I would like you both to be trained," she continued when I blinked at her, "and to help us in our hope of bringing our community back together."

God, this lady was smoking something nice.

"That's a pretty story, but you are delusional if you think that any of that will work that easy. I'd rather fight."

"Force rarely works the way you hope. I speak from experience."

"This time will be different."

"Shall we find out?" The queen smiled, holding her hand out to me, her palm glittering as water boiled through her flesh as though it had been hidden there. Rivers of clear blue water streamed over her hand, dripping to the floor in glistening drops that reflected a million colors I had never seen before. Even the water looked like magic, magic that was lifting from her skin and building into a pillar.

A pillar of water.

"What the hell are you doing?" I had seen magic. Hell, I had magic. But I wasn't sure what this was, or even if it qualified as magic. Didn't help that Queeny over here was smiling like a lark.

"Go ahead, touch it," she nodded toward the water, the dark sheen that was smothering her eyes making it clear I didn't have a choice.

My fingertip had barely tapped the swirling sides of the pillar when fire moved over my skin, seeping into my bones as flesh and veins boiled.

"Fuck!" I shrieked, holding the bubbling flesh of my finger against my chest. That water hadn't just burned me, it had boiled my skin.

I pressed myself to the wall, needing to get as far away from her and the water that was now shifting and bubbling like it was boiling. Like it was alive. Swirls of color moved over the surface of the pillar, shapes and colors forming until it was looking back at me.

No, I was looking back at me.

The little pillar of water had my fucking face on it. Smiling. Laughing. Battling against some guy with shaggy black hair, magic streaming from my fingers that looked nothing like it did now.

All of it while wearing the ugly as sin uniform from Imdalind Academy. The future. She was showing me the freaking future.

"Is this going to happen?" I asked, unable to tear my eyes away from the still shifting images.

"Your past defines your future, if you will allow it room in your soul." Her voice had changed, deepened into something hollow and terrifying. Just like her.

Her eyes were pure black. No silver, no white, just frightening demonic black as the water shifted to more images of a school, of that same shaggy black-haired boy, and a girl with a face covered with blood.

Her I recognized. The girl from the Gauntlet. She had tried to kill my friends, so in return I had placed my blast perfectly around her. Teach her a lesson.

"Enemies will abound in a world of skills and allies that appear where you least expect it..."

Scary dark voice or not, I already knew she was wrong. There was no way I was buddying up with that bitch, even if she had survived. Thankfully the image shifted to something that looked like a bloodied hand and a horrified face before it was gone and the last of the water splashed to the floor.

I shrieked and dodged away. No way in hell I was touching that stuff again.

"What the fuck are you, lady?" I shrieked, trying my best to move through the wall and away from her. Thank god her eyes had gone back to silver.

"I'm a Drak."

"Drak's are apparently much more frightening than the stories give you credit for."

She smiled at me, "Perhaps that's why I don't let stories get out."

Was that a threat? It didn't seem like it with how she was smiling at me, but I certainly wasn't going to start spreading rumors about the crazy queen any time soon.

Not with how she was looking at me.

"What do you say, Gemma? Will you join us at Imdalind

Academy? Will you help us build our world into something better?"

I had a feeling our ideas of 'better' were vastly different.

"What's in it for me? What's in it for my people?"

"A better world." She was dead serious, and I laughed in her face.

"That's just delusions speak when people are starving and sleeping on rags. You can do better."

"We can. And we will. Give us a chance, Gemma. Join us."

I really didn't want to trust her. I had come here to end her. Instead, I was cowering on the floor, my back against a wall.

"I suppose I can't really say no, can I?"

"You can, but I have a feeling you want to see what that future holds as much as I do. That and if you say no, I'll lock your magic."

"Lock my magic?"

"Yes. Permanently restrain it with an unbreakable bind."

Damn. So, I could either have her restrict my magic and go to school. Or have her remove it completely.

There was only one option.

Which was fine with me. She may have backed me into a corner, but there was a door in that corner, I would still figure out how to blow the place up.

I gave her a nod, staring at the drops of water that were slowly absorbing into the stone.

Nothing had changed. I wanted to end this monarchy, to end the tyranny against my people. I wanted to turn this world on its head. But she was right, I also really wanted to see what the future was.

Because I was pretty sure that that last image was my bloodied hand, wrapped around Prince Ryland's neck.

8

ROWAN

ANGIE WAS PERCHED ON THE EDGE OF HER SEAT, STARING THROUGH the wide glass window. Her little jaw was clamped tightly as she leaned closer, eyes wide at the beds that were covered with moaning, writhing people. Smears of blood and dirt covered everything so thick the entire room looked like one big crimson stain.

Through it all zipped the Skříteks, our family, and anyone with enough power to heal the wounded. Thank god the girl's misaligned attack had happened someplace full of magic strong enough to stitch skin and bones back together with ease. That, and that she had been unskilled enough to do much more than explode stone. I would have hated to see what she could do with more training.

"We really should head back to Imdalind, Ang," I said for probably the third time, not that I wanted to leave. I'd rather be down there, helping. Searching.

My mother was insistent I remained up there, however. So, I was stuck before the painted macabre with a sister as stubborn as I was.

I didn't see much of what was going on, I was still staring at the door they had pulled the girl through a few minutes before. She had been unconscious, a few of the Undermortals I had seen in my dream escorted in right behind her. They had gone in hours ago, and no one had come out.

Tension was wrapped around my spine like panic ready to strike. I shouldn't be worrying for her; she could clearly take care of herself after all. But after watching her in my dreams for so long, after failing to stop her from doing the unthinkable, I couldn't help but feel that I knew her. That I wanted to protect her.

Silly, really. But the thought didn't leave…

Another scream made me jump in my chair, pulling me away from the door and back to the twisted, bloody, carnival. This was no place for a child.

"Let's go, Ang." She shook her head, eyes still focused through the glass at all the writhing, screaming bodies.

It was possibly the only thing that was the same about this scene.

Normally this room, and its massive privacy glass, served as a kind of twisted viewing area. We would sit here, year after year, as the new Chosen crossed the finishing line to their new life.

It always struck me as odd that we would watch as they screamed and writhed from their bite. More than a few people had to be tied down to their bed before the magic overtook them and they fell into a deep sleep. Watching it every year, made me grateful that I had been born with my magic.

How long they slept determined how powerful their magic was and after a few hours the room would drift into silence, the Skřítek nurses finally allowing the families in.

The whole thing was creepy when you got right down to it. But I would take that to this any day.

The newly bitten chosen had been swept away to underground caves of Imdalind hours ago. It was only the mortals left. The children of the Chosen lying right beside the Undermortals like the equals they were supposed to be.

I was sure this wasn't what my father had in mind when we had wanted to unite the people.

"Angie, don't you think--?"

"I'm not supposed to leave yet," Angie said with that tone that I had always associated with a Drak, and therefore never used myself. "You can though. I know you want to help."

I gave her a look. She knew full well that my helping was consisting solely of making sure she didn't get in trouble.

"I won't go down there, Rowan." She gave me an exaggerated sigh and sat back in her chair, swinging her legs in a move that was way too cheerful for the horrors that were around us.

"Sure, you won't." I closed my eyes and leaned back in my chair.

Screams and moans and the rogue shout in Czech echoed through the glass, turning the tiny room into a buzz of energy. No, a buzz of magic. Magic that dripped in the air and whispered over my skin, pooling in the back of my neck in a warmth that was nearly begging me to follow it. To see, to really see.

My mother was pulling sight.

Real sight.

Not just the peeks into past and future that she normally did. Someone had touched Black Water. It had been ten years, but I would never forget that feeling. The power, the way light and time pulled through me as though you could reach out and touch it.

My chair banged to the ground as I jumped up, hands pressing against glass as my spine straightened, magic twisting through my bones as I stared at the door.

All I would have to do was close my eyes and I could see everything. It would take nothing to give into that side of me, to become that part of me. To grab the mug again and make that choice.

I turned, curious if Angie felt the same. But she just sat. Serene. Perfect. Happy.

Alive.

No. I would never let that magic fill me again.

Not now. Not ever.

If only for her.

I breathed a low sigh of relief when the magic finally abated, the warmth fading away and leaving me gasping against the window like a fish caught in a tank. I couldn't suck in enough air.

"Row?" Angie's voice was soft, the whisper far away and not just a few feet from where I stood. "Are you okay?"

I didn't turn. I didn't dare. I had no way of knowing what state my eyes were in and it wasn't worth the risk.

Thankfully, the door on the other side of the auditorium opened before I could gasp enough air to respond. Mother, Father, and a few of their guard whipped from the hallway and back into the massacre, all of them surrounding one painfully familiar, and exceptionally smug face.

She was alive.

I hated that it made me happy.

My parents were more apt to offer her a job and take her under their wing than sentence her. But from what I had seen of her, and how hard Talon had hit her, I half expected her to go into some kind of suicide mission.

She still might with how she walked, nose in the air, eyes darting around the room like an animal in a cage.

My fists clenched against my jeans, jaw tightening with each step they led her toward the other end of the hall. Where the buses were waiting to take her away.

Perhaps forever. I couldn't lose this.

I swallowed, magic prickling as I tore through the door, yelling something about 'staying there' to a smiling Angela.

I tore down the ornate steps and into the overfilled room, frantically searching for where they had gone. From this angle, however, the room was a sea of hair and blood. I could sooner find a pink mohawk as I could a Vilỳ.

Being locked up in our tiny observation tower had not prepared me for the smell of blood and vomit that drenched the air, for the heat of hundreds of bodies that sweated the air. My head was swimming, heart thundering and before I had thought better of it, I smashed my magic into me, wind bustling as I prepared to take off into the air and track them down.

"What in the world do you think you are doing?" Dramin snapped in my ear, his wide hand wrapping around my wrist and slamming me back down to the ground.

My brother glared at me, the wind falling to nothing as his magic smothered mine. Everyone frantically rearranged blankets, bandages, and the healing leaves. Side glances and mumbles followed us as Dramin pulled me away, his own curses mumbled between clenched teeth.

"I need to find her." I tried to break free of him, his usual passive face breaking into a wide smile.

"What have you seen baby brother?"

"Hellfire! Has she told everyone?" I yanked my hand away from his, ready to take off toward the shadow of my mother's magic.

"I'm assuming you mean our mother, and *she* has told me nothing." A tiny smile was playing at the corner of his mouth, his soft blue eyes completely out of place amongst the screams.

I could never tell if he was being facetious or not and now was not the time to play his weird games.

"Sure she hasn't," I snapped, taking a step back before I lost track of her magic altogether. "I need to stop her."

"Do what you need, but stay on the ground, Rowan. Now is not the time for dramatics. I dare say we have enough of that already." Dramin rushed one way with little more than a nod, leaving me to wind my way through the panic on my own.

Skříteks, Chosen, and even some Goldens wandered every which way, creating a forest of bodies that was moving in the opposite direction I needed to go. I pushed myself against the tide, sneakers slipping on the layer of wet that covered everything.

People ran, they pushed, they cried, they screamed, and I was sure I was getting absolutely nowhere.

"Move your fucking asses," I grumbled under my breath, shoving my way past a bandage laden Skřítek and toward the door that the faint whisper of my mother's magic was concealed behind.

I was steps away.

"What are you doing down here?" I was stopped for a second time when Talon intersected with me, fingers twisting around the collar of my shirt as he dragged me through the last of the crowd and toward the corner of the makeshift hospital. No one noticed either of us, Talon could have been carrying me to the slaughter for all they knew. The shadowy corner didn't help with that illusion. At least I could hear him over there, plus it also gave me a straight shot to the door, and my mother. Except that both my parents were now leaving the room, and the girl was not with them.

I could make it there if Talon would stop dragging me around like I was a child.

"Damn it, Talon, let me go. You are being ridiculous."

"I'm the one being ridiculous? You are the one who left our baby sister alone when we are under attack," he spat, shoving me against the wall as he let me go. Thankfully the floor wasn't as slick here or I would have fallen on my ass. The look he gave me made it clear that was his intention.

"We aren't under attack," I grumbled, rubbing my head as my magic sparked over the bruise I would have gotten from my impact with the wall.

"Oh really? Then what do you call this, dip shit? A Drain set off a bomb, and hundreds of our people are bleeding out, while more than a hundred Drains finished the Gauntlet and sit all nice and pretty in Imdalind. The last place they should be. This was a coordinated attack."

I glared at him. Drain. He spat the word around like poison. It twisted in my stomach.

"It wasn't coordinated..." I stopped midsentence, not really wanting to get into it right now. Dramin knowing about me was one thing. Acknowledging that Talon knew what I was, no, what my blood was, was as uncomfortable as the slur in the air.

"What are you doing down here, Rowan? What are you doing *here*?" He glared at the same door I had been trying to make it to, his eyes narrowed as though it had personally offended him.

"I need to talk to her." I didn't dare say much more than that.

"You were supposed to--" he stopped. He was staring at the same door I had been trying to make it to eyes narrowed as though it had personally offended him. "Her? You mean the girl?"

My stomach twisted as Talon's lip pulled into a sneer.

"Yes." I snarled, slipping out from where Talon had cornered me and returned to my attempt at the door. I didn't get more than a few steps before he was in front of me again. "I don't have time for this, Talon. I need to see her before it's too late."

"You think I'm going to let you waltz away from me?" His wide frame towered over me, his magic pulsing through the air right alongside his anger. His eyes narrowed, his macho-man brain making the connection a second before I was able to weasel my way past him.

"Let me go, Talon." The words squeaked out right before his magic wrapped around me, holding me in place and sucking the air from my lungs. "I thought you wanted me to go back to Angie?"

"You were going to the Drain." He glared at the door the second I did, although at this point it looked as bare and forgotten as the rest of them, no sign of what lay on the other side. "And I have a feeling you weren't going to kill it."

It. Both my anger and magic flared at that, my hand flexing as a single spark of white flew right into my brother, knocking the wind out of him, and giving me a thankful gasp of air. It had been his favorite trick since I was old enough to counter it. Not that it made it any better.

"It? What the fuck is wrong with you Tal?"

"Wrong with me? Look around you, shit head. They tried to kill our people!" He gestured around himself so wildly that he looked like Angela when Dad was teaching her to fly last year. The memory did little to calm the boiling fury that was moving through my veins.

He was acting more like a shit-head than I ever was.

"They are all our people, Talon. The Undermortals, the Chosen, the mortals," I cringed, realizing for the first time that both titles for those that lived underground were a bit derogatory. "All of them."

"You know, for all of your talk about not representing your birthright, you sure have taken a nice long drink of Dad's politics." He scowled, stepping closer to me until we stood toe to toe, magic sparking in the air between us as the lone light above started to flicker.

"Up until a few minutes ago I could have sworn you had too."

Talon sighed, running his hand through his hair as the bulb above us continued to flicker. I didn't dare move.

"I have, Rowan. I am with him on this." He was speaking through a tick in his clamped jaw, his eyes narrowed so severely that I was having a hard time believing him. "I'm with you, with Mom. But we have to think of this logically. We need to be united, but that means that some Drai--Undermortal who fell into a Vilỳ can't come and beat the shit out of us, either. Come here."

Talon's magic flared, his grip tightening as he pulled me further into the dark our parents had been heading toward. Our parents, Aunt Wyn, Uncle Ryland, and Aunt Mira stood around a bed, the sheets and floor so blood covered I was certain Aunt Wyn's magic was the only thing keeping whoever laid there alive. I could taste the sulfur of Wyn's magic even from here.

"See her?" Talon nodded toward the bed as Wyn shifted, the blood-soaked girl barely visible behind the vice-grip Wyn had on her shoulder. "She's the one who saw that Drain use her magic. She was right there, and she tried to stop it."

I recognized her at once, even with the bandages. It was the same girl from my dream, but whatever had happened, hadn't gone down anywhere near what Talon was claiming. She hadn't tried to stop anything. She had egged the Undermortal on.

"Sia Demarco. The eldest daughter to one of the most prolific Chosen families in our region." He, of course, didn't have to tell me that. Just the name and I knew who she was. And what her parents were.

Big old pains.

Our parents complained about Giovanni Demarco enough, fitting with the way the man strutted through the halls of Imdalind on more than one occasion.

"Can you imagine what the Chosen will do when they hear that their places in Imdalind Academy were taken by Drains, and that the girl who tried to stop it, the girl who almost died was the daughter of their elected voice in the monarchy." He was hissing in my ear, leaning closer to me as she turned to face me.

Her eyes had been hard and dark in my dream, the anger and vitriol seeping from her. The pain and sadness she fixed me with now, however, made it hard to believe it was the same girl. She smiled, the shy grin playing into the beauty I was sure she possessed when she wasn't covered with blood.

"If we want to unite our people, both Chosen and Drains have to be behind it. If they are attacking each other, that's not going to happen. The best thing you can do right now is to show the Chosen what they mean to us. The Drains are already at the academy, that's a start. But the Chosen need to know they still hold their place. That starts with this girl."

"I don't see what she had to do with me. We are standing in a hall full of blood..."

"I am trying to show you why your role at the Academy matters, and why you need to leave the Drains alone." His grip on my arm tightened, his fingers digging into my skin as little pricks of magic moved into me. They were clearly meant as more than a warning.

"Let me go, Talon. And stop using that word," I snapped, pulling my arm away from him, and away from the now boring stare of the girl.

I had seen that look before, it followed me around anytime I went to a public appearance. Even before then I had seen it in the eyes of every Chosen girl that Talon crossed paths with. Sia Demarco had more on her mind than 'being my friend.'

I wasn't interested.

Besides, I still had somewhere I needed to be.

"That Drain attacked you too, you know," Talon said, halting my escape, although I didn't turn. "That attack was on the royal family. She doesn't want to kill Chosen; she wants to kill

Eternals. Us. Mom. Dad. Ryland. Angela. Get your priorities straight and start thinking like a Krul."

"My priorities are straight." I dug my fists into my jeans, part of me questioning if they were.

If standing in a room full of injured people, trying to find the girl who hurt them was really the smartest thing. And not for the son of the King. For anyone.

"Sure you are, Rowan. You'll find out soon enough."

"What do you mean?" I asked, glancing behind me.

"Dad decided to lock that Drain up in Imdalind Academy with you, Row. That'll help remind you what they really are."

I whipped around, but Talon only smiled, laughed once and walked away, right toward a few other injured Chosen who had been staring at him. I didn't move. I stood, frozen in the shadows between the door that the uncomfortable whispers of sight that were pulling me towards and the gaze of the blood covered girl.

"I never asked for this."

9

____

SIA

"This group is fine, there are a few broken bones in the back, but I sent some of the Skříteks to heal them. They may be whining like spoiled brats, but they will be fine. Did you get them?" A woman's voice swam through the buzzing sound that was cleaving my head into two uneven halves.

Ripping everything in half.

High pitched ringing rattled against bones that felt splintered and broken, as though the shards were stuck out at odd angles. Okay, so I had no way of knowing if it was that bad, I couldn't see anything beyond the painful yellow glow of the most fluorescent sun in existence.

Something heavy was covering my face, smothering both the incessant buzzing that was trying to explode against my skull and the screams and yells that were filling the cave.

"Hello?" The one word question caught in my swollen throat, filling my mouth with blood and sending a new wave of pain over me.

I guess moving was out too, the agony was too much. Even if I tried, I couldn't lift so much as a finger.

It was like I had been hit with a bomb.

A bomb.

That girl, the one with the mohawk. The last thing I remembered was the sparks dripping from her fingers like jelly. Liquid lightning, just like the illegal, uncentered, magic that we had learned about in school back when they had taught us about the war. But that was impossible. They had captured all the Vilÿs and reserved power for those who won the Gauntlet, not some punk Drain that was inside of it.

I needed to get out of here, tell someone, warn them. Find her so they could execute her before she caused more damage. If they wouldn't kill her because of their damn morals or whatever, I would.

I tried to shift my weight, and push myself to sitting, but the best I got was rolling over. The cloth that had been covering my head slid to the slick tile floor with a slap, the blood-stained fabric followed by a stream of vomit that sent whoever had been rushing toward me back, the green and red splattering over the toes of their black converse shoes.

"This is really not how I saw this day going. Nasty." The same woman from before spoke from above me, but I didn't dare move. Not that I was sure I could, even the dim reflective light from the floor was increasing the crippling agony. Whoever that was better take a step back, more sick was coming.

Thankfully, my stomach was empty. Bits of bile splattered over the ground before I was forced onto my back, blinking furiously at the long fluorescent light above me.

The cave had gone, replaced by so much light that if it wasn't for blood, vomit, and smoke I might have thought I died. That, and the pain. I was in so much pain I didn't even realize I was laying on a soft feather bed.

Soft feather bed.

Oh god.

The hospital they took the losers too.

I can't have lost, not after all that. My father was going to be furious, and hopefully not at me.

"If you are going to do that again, roll over the other way and aim for the red sneakers. I like my shoes. I've had them for a few centuries and they don't make them like this anymore." The woman spoke again, her shoes squeaking against the tile floor as she came around the side of my bed, each step splintering my bones.

Damn this pain, I couldn't push past it, but I sure wasn't going to show it.

"Did you catch her?" I tried to ask, but the words came out all garbled, more blood filling my throat. Blood and vomit. I couldn't breathe.

"Hold still," the woman grumbled, a palm spreading square in the middle of my forehead, her fingers tapping against my nose. The pressure was making my head spin, my stomach lurch, and I gagged.

"Remember what I said about the red shoes, kid," she said, still tapping my nose.

"Why are you assuming that I don't like my shoes?" A deep male voice barked back as the woman's hand grew very warm. Warm and comfortable.

Like a hot water bottle that was radiating through my veins, my muscles. I had felt something similar when my mother would use her magic to heal me, but this was stronger, more powerful. More like fire.

Real magic. Eternal magic.

I tried to turn to see who was there, who was touching me, but her hand gripped tighter, her palm spreading over my eyes as she held me in place.

"It's not that you don't like your shoes, Thom. It's that I don't like your shoes. You look like..."

"Don't say it." The man, Thom, warned. The slight laugh in his voice was out of place.

"You need a feather hat." I could hear the laugh in her voice as he sighed, the sound cut off by more footsteps, these ones didn't rattle my bones as much.

She was so much more powerful than I expected the Eternals to be.

"Can I get an update?" The new voice said, this one familiar. This one I had heard on the radio and on TV so often that I probably could have picked it out of a crowd.

The King's brother, Ryland.

I tried to turn, but the warm-handed woman held me down harder, the heat from her hand growing.

"The cave is clear," The gruff-voiced Thom began. "We moved everyone who had already been bitten to the Academy to clear beds here. We've got Etma and the other Skříteks healing and releasing those with minor cuts or broken bones. Jos mentioned something about transporting the worst ones to Imdalind, so we moved them together..."

"And this one?" Ryland cut Thom off, and every single one of my muscles tensed, thankfully not feeling like they were going to snap like a rubber band inside of me. I was sure he was talking about me.

"Alive, but it was touch and go there for a bit." The woman said, all humor from before gone. "She's awake now so I would go get them so we can question her before we get her bitten and off to Imdalind. Did you guys get a hold of her parents?"

"Unfortunately. Do you know whose daughter this is?" There was a pause, my heart swelling as I prepared for the awe and respect that usually came with my family name. That would fix this. "She's a Demarco. They are already here."

"Shit. I'll go speak to them," Thom said as more footsteps cut through the mumbling cries of pain from the other victim.

I was no longer so sure they were talking about me. Touch and go? Add such disdain with my name? Ridiculous. The conversation around me no longer made sense, especially now that most of the pain was gone.

I had no interest in laying here in confusion, I needed answers. But, even without pain, I wasn't moving, no matter how hard I tried. Didn't help that the woman's palm was now fully covering my face, the warm weight holding me down.

"Seriously, kid, stop moving." The lady said, tapping her fingers over my cheekbone now. "You are going to hurt yourself."

"Perhaps if she could see she wouldn't be fighting you so much." Ryland's voice was as I had always heard it, strong, powerful, and perfectly correct.

I didn't know who this bitch was, but this was the closest I had ever been to any of the Eternals. Ryland was right there and I didn't need one of the Skřítek guards to be keeping me from him. Injured or not this wasn't an opportunity I planned on wasting. I shifted my weight again and tried to say something that ended up being nothing more than bubbles of drool and blood that drizzled out of the corner of my mouth.

That got her to move.

"Yeah, well, she probably needs to sit up if we are going to get anything other than blood out of her," The woman said as her hand shifted to my collar bone, the radiating heat moving with her. "But I don't dare move her until Jos gets here. She threw up a minute ago and fractured another bone in her spine. Add that to the ruptured kidney, a punctured lung, and half a dozen broken bones. A fractured spine is nothing!"

"Fractured?" The word was bubbles of panic and I instantly tried to shift again, my eyes furiously blinking as they tried to adjust to the blinding yellow glow of the fluorescent light.

"Oh, hold up," she said, her wobbly shape hovering over me

as what looked like grey smoke shrouded us, dimming the light and pulling her into focus.

It wasn't some dumb guard. It was Wynifred. Thomas's wife. Cail's mother. I was surrounded by not one, but two of the royal family. Three, as I suddenly realized that Thom was short for Thomas.

Holy sh--

"Ha-ha, will you look at that, she recognizes us," Wynifred said with a smile that wrinkled around her dark eyes.

"Either that or she is horrified because you told her that her back is fractured," Ryland said, leaning over me from the other side.

Oh god, his eyes were even bluer from close up. I couldn't look away, the light sky blue was like pools among his dark hair, pulling me in. I could only hope that Rowan's eyes were as stunning.

"Naw, I've seen that look before." Wynifred waved her free hand to the side as Ryland stepped out of my line of vision. I tried to turn but nothing happened, well nothing but a lightning bolt of pain down my spine. I winced.

"What is going on?" Again, the words were unintelligible, although thankfully there wasn't quite as much drool that time.

"Screw it. If this hurts kid, don't worry. I'll heal it, or cauterize it, or whatever I need to. I'm sure you have questions, so do we, and we need to have this conversation quick so we can get your magic awakened and send you off to Imdalind so you can heal the right way."

Imdalind. She hadn't said the Academy, just Imdalind. The underground city where the royals lived, where magic comes from. Where I would live one day. Soon.

Images of a beautiful homecoming were wiped clean when a wind wrapped around me, lifting me to sitting as both mattress and pillows were lifted and lodged behind me to keep me upright. The motion ripped me apart, my joints and bones screaming as they twisted and moved in ways I was sure they weren't supposed to. I grit my teeth, desperate to keep my scream inside, but it ripped its way out, splattering blood over the white sheet and buzzing in my head.

Screaming made everything worse. I had never felt anything like this before, and I had put myself through hell preparing for the Gauntlet. This felt like all my bones were on the outside instead of the inside.

Heaving, I grit my teeth and locked the scream inside. Stubbornly refusing to face any of the Eternals as anything less than what I was.

I would not scream again.

Besides, Ryland and Wynifred were not the only ones here.

Mira stood not too far off, eyes bouncing between me and the dozens of other moaning, blood-soaked people in the beds around us. Dozens of us had all been caught up in whatever that girl Gemma had done, although none of them were screaming. None of them had their own entourage of Eternals, either.

That entourage was about to get bigger.

The King and Queen were headed my way.

Ilyan and Joclyn weaved their way through the rows and rows of beds, tapping the metal frames of those who were still unconscious. They glanced between each one, mumbling about who knows what as they came closer.

As they walked right up to me.

Ilyan towered over Joclyn, their jackets and perfectly tailored trousers stained with blood and dirt. Joclyn even had a massive hole in the knee of the once black fabric. They were beautiful, elegant, and even with the pain I sat up as best as I could to watch them, to watch the long golden ribbons of their crowns twist around each other from the tips of their braids.

"Beautiful." Of course, that was the first thing I said that made any sense.

"Yeah, you say that now," Wynifred gave me a wink and put her warm hand back on my shoulder, the palm hot against my bare skin thanks to a massive hole in my shirt. I was actually amazed the thing was held together as well as it was.

Oh well, I had bought the thing last week and had already worn it once before, it was due to be tossed anyway.

"How is she?" The queen asked in a voice so windy that I almost didn't recognize it as the powerful woman from before the gauntlet.

It was only her voice that was calm, however. Everything else about her screamed of power, the way she stood, the dark glint in her silver eyes as they looked right at me, through me maybe. It was hard to tell. Hell, it was hard to breathe underneath that look and I fell back against the pillows with a gasp.

"Well, you know, I've seen worse. She'll be fine, but I think you're right about the bite..." Wynifred's rambling was cut off as Mira stepped up to Ryland, clearing her throat and giving the woman a glare like I had never seen before.

Oh. My. God. They were everywhere. Mira and Ryland on one side, Wynifred on the other and the freaking King and Queen right in front of me. I didn't know where to look.

"Fine. Fine." Wynifred said, clearing her throat. "My lord, my lady, this is Sia Demarco. She is the witness to the attack. Miss Demarco, I give you the King and Queen."

Everything in my life had been leading up to this moment. This moment was nothing like I had imagined it. I was not being praised for completing the Gauntlet first, nor was their son anywhere around and wearing a tuxedo. I was covered with blood, my hair a mess, and I wasn't even sure that I could form coherent words without bleeding all over myself.

Still, I was going to try.

"Your Majesties." It was mostly understandable, and thankfully limited with the blood and drool combo. The head bow, however, didn't move beyond an inch, but they didn't seem to notice.

"It's nice to meet you, Sia. Although I wish it had been in better circumstances," Ilyan began, stepping closer to the bed and blocking my view of the Queen. "Judging by your injuries it appears that you were the lone witness to the attack. We believe we have the attackers in custody and have been speaking to others involved, but we are hopeful that you can give us the information we need."

"I will be of as much assistance to you as I am able." It was getting easier to speak, thank god. It was going to be impossible to create the right impression if I had blood oozing from the corner of my mouth.

I tried to bow again, that time my head moved a fraction of an inch. It barely hurt, although I was sure that was from Wyn's burning palm against my shoulder, and her magic that was quickly turning me into a furnace.

"Good to hear," Ilyan gave me a smile. "Can you tell us what you saw?"

"There were these Drains... Mortals..." I quickly corrected when Wynifred's hand tightened on my shoulder. "They were in the last room, the one without light."

"How many were there?" Ilyan prompted, his voice growing to the same deep tone as before the doors had opened, the rumbling baritone shaking the broken bones in my back. A tiny shadow of pain rippled up my spine and I cringed, prompting another wave of heat to radiate from Wynifred's hand. I didn't want to see what condition my shoulder would be in after this.

"Seven, maybe more."

"What happened?" They all leaned in at Ilyan's question, except for Mira who took a step back, going into guard mode.

God. I was broken to bits and I still wanted nothing more than to be like her.

"I saw them huddled around one of those cards, they were talking about the end and some plan. I didn't have ti--" I paused, my heart thundering as I lay there. Wynifred's warmth cascaded through me, weird pricks running up my spine that almost felt like my bones were piecing themselves back together.

I wanted this. I wanted this power. To be among them. This was my place, and there was only one way I was going to get there.

"I didn't know what they were talking about," I continued, clearing my throat to make up for the pause. "But there was something about the way they were speaking that scared me. I didn't have much time, I know you only let so many into Imdalind Academy, and I waited to run, so this might be my only shot..." I paused again, adding a dramatic pout that may not have all been acting. "It was a risk, but I followed them, and when they started taunting others, threatening to throw them into a crevice; I fought them. I tried so hard to stop them. The others got free, but one of the girls with them fell in. The main girl, this girl with a pink mohawk, Gemma I think, she was pissed and tried to push me in too. But I ran, and then they caught up with me, and then..."

I sped up with each word until my voice caught and I heaved, trying to force in a shuddering breath. Okay, so maybe this super-magic healing hadn't reached there yet. That hurt. I gasped and winced undoing the dramatic impact I had been trying to make.

They were looking at me with pity.

The vile, disgusting look was not one I wanted.

"I tried to stop them, My Lord," I said softly, hoping to wipe the look from their faces. "I really did. That kind of thing... I can't believe it." Pause. Sniffle, I even tried to wipe my nose, not realizing my arm still didn't move. "Did many people get hurt?" Or rather, how many Drains got hurt. How many Drains were knocked out of the competition? "Did the gauntlet get called off?"

They all exchanged a look, looking from the King to me and back again, before Queen Joclyn stepped out around Ilyan's towering frame, a darkness fading from her eyes.

Just like before the doors to the gauntlet had opened. The Drak sight.

Oh lord. Had she seen something? Is that why she was hiding behind Ilyan and Mira had been looking at her like a hungry lioness? I had no idea how Drak magic worked, but if she saw both past and future like everyone had said then she could have seen right through me.

But then, if she had known, she wouldn't be smiling at me the way she was.

Maybe Drak's weren't as infallible as the books in school claimed.

Didn't matter, I couldn't take back what I had said, might as well amp it up.

"Did everyone make it out alive?" I added a pout to that since I still couldn't move my arms.

"The Gauntlet completed before the explosion, thankfully," Joclyn began, still fixing me with that smile.

A damn ugly smile that burned as bad as what she had said.

"The Gauntlet was completed?"

"Yes, all the spots had been filled minutes before."

My heart sunk, the world shattered, Joclyn's continued explanation pounding against the back of my fractured skull while the word *'failure'* buzzed like an alarm.

No. It couldn't be. There had to be a way I could salvage this. I couldn't be left a fecking Tarn.

"Not many were left in the final task. The injuries were

limited. You seem to have caught the brunt of it as you were right before this girl, Gemma, you said?"

"Yes, that's what they called her. I am so glad she and her people didn't hurt more. I am so glad I was able to delay her from her plans, so that it wasn't worse." That was the closest thing to the truth I had said all night.

"Did you see how she made the explosion?"

It felt like she was looking through me again. Not only was it creepy as hell but it was sincerely making me question the last few minutes. Before now I probably would have made up some story of a bomb. I had planned on it. But the truth fell out as if it was pulled there, even my voice shook.

God, what was her magic doing to me? It had to be her magic, there was no other explanation.

"Magic. I could have sworn she had magic. That drippy stuff we saw in the videos or in safety drills back in primary school."

Joclyn nodded, her penetrating silver glare finally pulling away and looking from me, to Ilyan. He didn't seem fazed. The two stared at each other like they were mind melding, their lips pulling up at the exact same moment before Joclyn strode off back the way she came, Mira taking off after her like she was on a string.

Fecking hell, maybe Drak's could read minds. Was that what she had been doing to me? I really hoped not, but the creepy showdown wasn't giving me much hope.

"What's going on?" Each word caught in my throat. I wasn't even sure I wanted to know.

"The Queen has matters to attend to," Ilyan said, taking a wide step toward the foot of the bed. The King's stare was calming in comparison to his wife's. Probably thanks to the color of his eyes. "We thank you for your assistance in this matter, Miss Demarco. As we said, the Gauntlet had finished minutes before the attack, but with what you went through, and the injuries you have sustained, we have decided to give you an honorary place in Imdalind Academy and will administer the bite as soon as you are ready. The bite of the Vilỳ will not only awaken your magic, but assist you in healing better than any of us can."

I hadn't failed after all. I still had a place. It may not be first, it may have been last, but it came with honors. It came with recognition and my first meeting with the people with which I truly belonged.

I nodded once, ignoring the pain that ripped over my spine with the motion.

"Thank you, My Lord, and give my thanks to My Lady as well."

"I will," Ilyan said with a nod.

"I do not deserve such an honor." Tears, real honest tears were dripping down my cheeks and I looked from the king, to Ryland, to Wyn, to the boy that stood off in the shadows with Talon, his dark eyes trained right at me.

Rowan.

He was here. He was right here, and he was looking at me.

"I will make you proud, my King," I lifted my voice as loud as I could, giving Rowan a prolonged stare before I turned to his father, forcing my arm to lift as I bore my bare wrist to the King, the wrist that would normally receive the bite. "I will serve you and your family in any way I can. It's an honor."

Humble. Obedient. But instead of a smile, I was met with a scoff from the very boy I had been trying to impress.

"Be honest and forthright to yourself, and you will make yourself proud," Ilyan said with a rumble. He gave me one tiny nod before he turned, beckoning Ryland after him with a wave as they bee-lined right to where Rowan stood.

"I'll send someone over, Wyn. Don't do anything I wouldn't do," Ryland said before he took off after the King, leaving

Wynifred and I alone, the heat in her hand slowly pulling back into her like it was an old-fashioned tape measure.

"Well, you're off to a rocky start," she mused, giving me a wink before she removed her hand from my shoulder, the last of the warmth leaving as all the pain from before came rushing back.

"What start?" I asked, the words swallowed in my throat as everything ripped to shreds and I fell back against the pillow, my head turning to the side, and to Rowan, who was still looking right at me.

Not one hint of joy on his face.

10

GEMMA

"Damn. Is this really how you live? I mean, I've seen worse. Especially right after the war, but I had assumed we had moved past this."

"You thought wrong," I interrupted the bubbly 'guard' that had been sent with me to collect my things and my 'one friend' before I was shipped off to Imdalind Academy.

Or, what I was officially referring to as magic hell.

Although, that started the second they had assigned her to escort me to and from what had always been home.

Eyes followed us through the filthy blankets and makeshift homes that littered the main hall of Last Pyre. It had always been safer to sleep together, but now I realized how bad of a choice that was. After the Queen had centered my magic and fixed whatever it was that was making me so tired, I had been locked in some weird hotel outside the Gauntlet to heal, rest, and *bathe* according to the snooty Skřítek that had taken me there. Which was all fine until we walked in here, into this wall of a stench that was nearing a level of harassment.

That I could deal with, though. The aroma was familiar. And as foul as it was, I didn't want to leave.

I would gladly take this against fancy hotels, running water, and something called a buffet that I had sat at and stuffed my face until I threw up. Which, when you got right down to it, was why I subjecting myself to all of the rules and regulations and fancy hotels. So that it all could be familiar to everyone.

They deserved that too. I was going to give that to them. The path to get there had changed, that's all.

Awe rippled through the mud streaked faces and hungry eyes as I walked through my home in search of the one person I was taking away from this mess.

"Gemma?" More than a few people whispered, shock radiating the air before they saw who I was with and more than a few Undermortals scuttled back into their makeshift homes, or out of the room altogether the look of fear, panic, and betrayal glancing back to me.

It was hard to be a bad-ass leader of the revolution when you were escorted by an Eternal. When you had brought an Eternal into the one place we were supposed to be safe.

Wynifred Krul was bright, overly happy, and quickly becoming a pain in my ass. If it wasn't for the faint outline of tattoos that lined the entire left side of her body, I would say she didn't fit in here at all.

"All of this," she continued, waving her hand in front of her. "This is balls. I'm going to fix it before it gets too gross and hairy, although it might already be there. I'm bringing food, speakers, and holding a Styx dance-off down here next week. Sorry you have to miss it, kid. It'll be epic." She threw her arm around my shoulder like we were some kind of squealy girlfriends. I shrugged it off. Chick was too far into my personal space.

"I don't know what in the world you are talking about, but there is no way anyone will come to a dance-up..."

"Dance-off," she corrected with a wink, the shadows of her tattoos wrinkling around her eyes.

"Whatever. That doesn't change anything. They aren't coming." I turned away from her, motioning at Eddy, who had strutted around the corner and froze, eyes popping out of his head at the sight of me and my rambling companion.

"And why won't they come? I throw a wicked party, trust me. My music may be three hundred years..."

"They don't trust you." I interrupted, tapping my foot and making eyes at Ed in an attempt to get him over here. The guy looked terrified.

"This guy trusts me," she said, nodding to Eddy who was slowly walking towards us. So slow he might as well have been walking backwards.

I gave her a look, my eyebrows twisting together. She beamed with a broader grin. Damn, all these Eternals were delusional.

"This guy is terrified you are going to eat him. Eddy?" I asked when he was only about half way too us. "Do you trust her?"

He froze in place, taking one slow step back.

"I don't know how to answer that. If I say no, will she kill me?" Poor Eddy was practically shaking in his boots. I didn't blame him, Wynifred had always been an unknown. I would have avoided her too. But then I was stuck with her prattling on about renegade magic for the past two hours while she drove us here. I was amazed to be in a car that nice, she wanted to lecture me on a hundred different ways to blow things up.

So yeah, I guess still terrifying. Just terrifying and irritating.

"I haven't killed anyone in a few hundred years, kid, and I used to be pretty good at it."

Eddy took another step back, a tiny squeak echoing from behind one of the tents in the communal sleeping space we were traversing through.

"You enjoyed blowing people up?" I asked, regretting the question when she smiled. Despite my rage against the

Demarco girl, had never killed anyone. Although my plans to do so had not changed, I sure as hell hoped I didn't look deranged when I talked about, like she did right now.

"You enjoy turning buildings to rubble," she shrugged, smiling again.

"I enjoy standing up to oppressors for the sake of my people." It was taking everything in me not to throw her into the wall. But I wasn't about to go throwing murderesses against walls if I wasn't sure I could win.

"The thing about causes, kid, is that you have to make sure you are on the right side. The bad side looks just like the good one when you don't know any better."

"I know which side I'm on," I said between the grit in my teeth, fists tight against my thighs. Maybe I could punch her.

"Sure you do, come find me after you've killed your third 'tyrant' and tell me if you still think so. Maybe we can go blow up buildings together. Or people. Guess it depends on how your revolution pans out." She looked around her, again. The curious under mortals who had peeked out to stare at us retreating back into their holes.

"What the hell is wrong with you?"

"Boredom." She shrugged her shoulders, the maniacal light vanishing from her eyes.

How in the hell was this a four-thousand-year-old immortal and mother of the headmaster to Imdalind Academy?

I couldn't wrap my head around it. This had to be some sort of a show, or every bit of reconnaissance we had done on the royal family was glaringly wrong.

I wasn't holding out much hope of any of it being true after my run in with Thomas and the Queen.

"Well, go be bored over there." I waved off in the direction of the toilets. "I need to talk to him." I knocked my head toward Eddy, the guy still trying to make an escape for it.

"Is he your choice, then? He looks fun. I like your shirt, dude. The Doctor is a classic."

Eddy jerked to a stop, all escape forgotten as his jaw sagged, "You know Doctor Who?"

"Hell, yeah! Everything 1970s is my jam." She pointed to her shirt and some weird montage of robots, as if we were supposed to know what that meant. "If you ever end up coming to Imdalind I'll show you a few episodes, I doubt you've got a ton of access to them down here."

"I finagled some stuff last year after I found a VHS and Gem was able to get it running. It was bad-ass."

"Well, if *Gem*," she gave me a wink on her discovery of my nickname. My blood was starting to boil. "If Gem brings you with her then we should totally plan something. Row--"

"Enough of this. I have things to do, and you have a dance-up to plan. Over there." I snarled, pushing myself between Wynifred and Eddy, giving the former a slight zap of warning. I didn't dare do the same to Wynifred seeing as she was bored and liable to kill people.

"It's a dance-off. An epic dance-off."

"You can't be for real," I hissed, she just laughed.

"Yeah, I get ya, too strong. I would turn on the other side of me," her tone dropped with that, laughter pulling to a halt as her eyelids drooped. Feet slid over stone as she stepped closer to me, fingertips running over my shoulders. I shivered, I honest to god shivered, and I almost slapped her for it. "But I don't want to scare you."

She lifted her hand, the exposed fingertips of her gloved hand hovering less than an inch from my face, flicking, moving as if they were touching me. I swear I could feel her magic, either that or the blood was boiling.

"There is darkness in the world, you know, it's often hidden behind the smiles, behind the joy that would mask it, just ready to strike."

It was clear she had used this trick before, that she expected me to cower and scuttle away like some obedient Undermortal.

Enough of this.

I laughed in her face, grabbing her hand and wrapping my fingers around her wrists, pulling her hand away from me. It wasn't just the air that was boiling.

Her skin felt like a freaking furnace.

I lifted my magic to match, not sure if it was doing the same thing before I shoved her away, sending her stumbling on her old ratty sneakers.

"Nice trick," I said, shock covering her face. Now it was my turn to smile. "Seems you lot are full of them. But I grew up here, and have been blowing up your precious stores for the past few months. Pretty sure you can't scare me."

"Was that a threat or a promise? Because I enjoy both," Wynifred said with a wicked grin, giving me a wink. "You have ten minutes and then I'm dragging your ass out of here."

Daggers flew between our glares, magic and threats assaulting before she turned toward the bathrooms that I had indicated. She only got about half way before she stopped to wave at the few people who were brave enough to peek out from their hiding places to see her.

I was suddenly glad the queen hadn't restricted my magic yet. I wasn't about to blow Wyn up, but it felt better knowing that I could if whatever darkness in her took control.

"What the hell was that?" Eddy hissed in my ear, staring at Wynifred who was now trying to coax a litter of kittens out of their home.

"*That* was another bit of crazy from a bag of rats that I seem to have accidentally opened." I sighed, running my hand over the shaved parts of my hair, and the old tattoo that was hiding underneath the prickles.

"Yeah, speaking of bags of rats," Eddy said, grabbing my forearm and pulling me away from the Eternal who was now conducting her own parade toward the bathrooms, complete with kittens and a few children. "What the hell happened in those caves? We all ran the second those Eternals started descending from the sky like some giant birds. One second you were there, next, you were carried off by that guy with the dreads."

"Thom," I corrected, realizing a second too late that I had. He gave me a look.

"You looked dead, Gem. We all thought you were dead."

Which explains most of the shocked looks that had followed us in.

"I don't think they ever planned on killing me. Or any of us. They say they want the same thing we do."

"Which is?"

"End to the class system. Equality. They want me to help them achieve it." Saying it aloud was twisting in my stomach, that flash of an image I had seen in the Queen's hand gnawing at me. This bag of rats was getting out of control.

"And you believe that?" His hushed whispers broke into a shriek, his hands flying into the air in frustration. Luckily the one woman parade that was still making her way to the bathroom hadn't noticed.

"About as much as I believe the psycho back there is going to show you some old television collection." His face fell. I shrugged. "Sorry, dude, it's the truth. I don't know what they are up to, but at this point I'd more trust the CCC to host a dance-up down here." Eddy gave me a look, I waved him off. "Doesn't mean I have a choice though..."

"Gemma?" Another whisper filtered around the corner as

Adrian, Aria, and a few other of my Undermortals froze after turning around the corner. There was a flash of shock in his face, and some confusion I didn't understand before he inhaled and bolted right to me. Adrian's tears dripping on my shoulder as he swept me up in his arms, muscles pressing me against him as he attempted to kiss me more than a few times.

Normally his touch was more of a numb nothing; there was no swoop of a stomach or twist of desire between us. This time, angry fury was rumbling through my veins. My magic was on a rampage, bubbles of hostility moving under my skin and sparking dangerously. I pushed him away, if only to save him before I hurt him. The second I did, the magic fell away, moving into an uncomfortable rumble at the contact.

What the fuck was that? My magic better not have turned into some kind of sentient being with her own taste in men, because that was so not going to fly with me.

"Oh baby, I thought you were dead." He smashed me against him again, oblivious to the danger he was in. After being around the pampered Eternals for the last few days I think I got my first good whiff of him.

Man, we all stunk.

"Seems to be a common theme," I said, grateful for the excuse to pull myself away again. "Not dead yet. I might be by the end of the year, though."

They all exchanged a look, and I took another glance at Wynifred, who Adrian thankfully hadn't noticed yet. I wasn't sure what he would do if he saw an Eternal here. The guy was more muscle then smarts and it made him fly off the handle dumb sometimes.

"What are you talking about?"

"They are enrolling me in Imdalind Academy." The reaction I got from that couldn't have been more varied. Most of them gasped, hands flying to mouth in shock. Adrian looked about ready to pop some heads off some Chosen, and Eddy, Eddy was chuckling.

"What in god's name are they thinking," Adrian snarled, pounding his fists together. "They can't take you away from me."

Yes, because that was the concern. My apparent hip attachment with him. He seriously needed to get a grip.

"They are thinking I either learn how to control my magic and bow to them, or they bind it and end our revolution right here and now," I said, ignoring Eddy's quizzical expression. He hadn't missed that I had omitted the whole 'working for them' thing. "But you can't tame a snake. You can tie it down. You can torture it. It will still bite you in the end. I don't see why I can't keep this fight going from within their walls."

"You are going to try to start a coup from inside of a school filled with Goldens, Chosen, and more than a dozen Eternal spawn? You have more of a death wish than I thought." Eddy chuckled like it was some kind of joke.

If he thought that was funny, then he was really going to hate what came next.

"More than a hundred of the new enrollees are Undermortals. The school is filled with our people ready to fight for our cause. Adrian, I need you to keep building up the next generation at home." I took one step toward Adrian. I was going to have to fan his ego if the guy was going to get over what I was about to do to him. "The Undermortals love you as much as I do. You will need time to reach out to the other communities and build an army while Eddy and I work from inside. We will take them down using their own--"

"You're taking Eddy with you?" Adrian interrupted me, his voice feral and frightening. So much for padding his over-inflated ego.

"I negotiated one additional enrollment; Eddy will be able too--"

"Eddy is a soft pussy who can't take a shit without help," Adrian cut me off again, shoving Eddy back and sending him stumbling toward one of the lean-to camps. He barely caught himself.

Adrian wasn't so lucky.

My newly centered magic went into overdrive, rumbling through my veins as a wind I hadn't known I could summon whipped around me, lifting me off my feet and bringing me right to Adrian's towering eye level. He didn't look nearly as imposing when facing him head on. Reaching my hand forward, his eyes widened as magic sparked and jumped between my fingers. No longer was it the drippy illegal stuff I had been using for years, but the clear brilliantly colored sparks of real magic.

Adrian looked at me with true fear for the first time.

"You don't get to interrupt me, Adrian." I snarled, his eyes widening as the lightning jumped from my fingers to snap above his head. "You don't get to question my choices. You are the one I have chosen to lead in my stead while I am at school taking them down from the inside. You don't trust me? You don't respect me? There are hundreds of others here who would want the job. But I chose you."

The whipping wind of my magic picked up, the lean-tos and blanket nests that covered the massive sleeping space rattling as dust and trash and everything else lifted up to surround us in our own little tornado of trash.

It was the least sexy thing I had ever been involved in. Adrian didn't agree, he was already looking at me like an animal, his pink tongue wetting his dry lips as he held my hips against his. Which was fine, made what came next easier.

"I want you." I pressed my wet lips to his dry ones, the magic falling from my fingers as I pressed my hand against his neck.

He sighed, his hands trailing down my spine to cup against my ass, pulling me into him. He groaned in desire, but I felt nothing but that same angry power buzzing through my veins. I wasn't sure if that was a good sign.

"If I didn't know you," he continued, "I would say they already have you under their spell, that you've already abandoned us."

"Good thing you know me then." I gave him another wink and another kiss. "I'd rather die than let them continue to rule over us. I will see them in a puddle of their own blood, screaming for mercy."

Just like that image in the Queen's hand.

"That's my girl," he grinned, forcing another kiss. I pulled away.

"So, will you help me then?"

Adrian's dark brown eyes narrowed, his brows pulling together in the look that I had always described as 'meat head concentration'. The name had never suited it more.

"Of course I will." He said it loud enough for everyone to hear before pulling me in and whispering in my ear. "And I'll keep our bed warm for you for when you return, as my queen."

My stomach flipped, but not for some exhilaration of some guy who thinks I'll be pining for his bed and some pet name he seemed to think I wanted. That was gross.

My stomach flipped for the Queen, the current one, and the burn that was still aching on the tip of my index finger.

Her superpowers were really putting a damper on our plan, and I hoped to shit she couldn't see this conversation or what we were planning. I really needed to find out how all of that worked.

"I'll be looking forward to it." I gave him a wink, enough to bolster his lusty ego back up to where it belonged and stepped away, right into a hard chest.

"Holy shit!" Adrian growled, his eyes narrowing at what I immediately registered as an attack.

"Tarns!" I yelled the warning, as I spun around, hands lifting as the magic that had once been weak and dripping exploding from me in a line of what looked like green smoke.

The powerful attack zoomed through the air as I bellowed a war cry, ready to destroy whatever had invaded us. It was a beautiful sight, the real magic, until it hit against an invisible wall with a blast that rattled the floor and shook the fragments of metal that hung from the ceiling. One of the ancient things collapsed to the ground, fire spreading from whatever I had hit, the air filling with harmless grey smoke and the crumpling sound of metal.

"Tarns!" I yelled again, hands still forward as the smoke cleared, ready to attack again.

"Crap, girl. You gotta learn how to control that." Wynifred stepped through the last of the smoke to face us. "You're gonna take out a monarchy if you're not careful."

Her eyebrows twisted dangerously as she stepped right up to me, the same frightening grin from before covering her face.

I knew that bubbling pain in my ass from before was a farce!

"Isn't that the point?" I stepped right up to her and she blew in my face, the smell of smoke on her breath, as though she was burning from the inside.

"That's up to you, Gem." God, I wish Eddy had never used that name around her. Let's hope she could keep it to herself.

"What is this? You let one of them in here? What are you playing at Gemma? What have you done?" Adrian's rage bubbled through the air, it rumbled in a warning that I had heard a few too many times.

The idiot was about to make a terrible mistake.

I let him.

I stepped to the side as he lumbered past me, right toward the Eternal who smiled as the same blast of flame erupted around her. Sparks flew as though she herself had erupted.

The fire hadn't burst from her hands however, it had come from the ground in front of her. Blankets, clothes, and someone's personal belongings mixed with the shattered stone as it all erupted into the air in a bomb that sent Adrian back, flying through the air and into the far wall with a loud thwack.

It was a blast like the ones I used to make, but instead of magic, it was flame, everything so perfectly controlled that the blast hadn't passed more than a foot in diameter. It shouldn't have even had the force to move Adrian anywhere, but he was already embedded into stone dozens of feet away.

"Holy shit," Eddy muttered, his eyes wide as he looked from the smug Wynifred to Adrian who was sliding down the wall like a puppet with cut strings.

"Sorry!" Wynifred yelled, that playful tone back as she waved to Adrian, who had landed on the floor in a wad. "No hard feelings! You scared me!"

Fitting, seeing as she scared everyone else.

The few that had been brave enough to poke their heads out were gone. The normally bustling living space was empty except for a few tendrils of smoke.

"You ready, Gemma?" Wynifred asked from somewhere behind me, her forced playfulness hollow against the emptiness of my home.

This was not the last memory I had hoped to have in this place.

Bleak. Broken.

I had to fix this.

That meant giving them the fuel to carry on without me.

Yes, Adrian looked ridiculous crumpled against the wall like he was. Ass in the air, forced to smell his own junk. But his face was full of rage, everyone else staring with fear.

Staring at her. At our enemy.

"Yeah, I'm ready," I whispered, pulling Eddy after me as we followed Wynifred out of our home.

I gave one last look at Adrian before I left, gave him one nod, and blew one lone kiss for good measure.

The rage on his face did not leave.

Perfect.

11

———

ROWAN

BLOOD DRIPPED FROM FINGERS, IT CLUNG TO WALLS, AND POOLED around my formerly white sneakers. It lay imprinted in scarlet prints on shoulders and arms that looked too close to desperate fingers. Reaching, pleading.

Screaming.

The sound, the color, the repeat of both sight and memory was everywhere. Blood coated the world as my own pulsed in my throat and made it hard to breathe.

This was not how I imagined my first time in Council.

There was only one room in Imdalind that I had never been allowed in, The Council Hall. Now that I was here, however, I wanted to turn right around and never return.

The room was beautiful, don't get me wrong, the tall ceilings, the old stone work that swept over the ceiling in ribbons and magic and leaves that looked to real to be only stone. But all of that stone was coated in dark stains that drizzled against the walls, slithered over the floor and covered the massive stage-like dais at the far end of the cavernous room that didn't look like mineral deposits. It was probably a trick of the light, or the fact that everyone that stood around me was coated in blood, but I was sure those dark stains over the stone were blood too.

I swallowed and stepped back from the rest, hovering with Talon, Dramin, and Patrice near the far wall where three chairs had been set up. We were present, but not included. The children of the King, but not rulers.

That role belonged to my Aunts and Uncles.

Mira, Ryland, Wyn, and my parents were all hovering around a giant piece of parchment that they had rolled out on the floor, pointing and talking while lines and dots moved between two points like it was some kind of magical ant hill. It took me a moment to realize what I was looking at: the body count. Well, I guess not 'bodies' seeing as no one had died, but all those squiggles and lines weren't necessarily the most positive depiction.

The pulse in my throat was getting worse.

"All of those who completed the Gauntlet and received their bite before the explosion were successfully moved to the main hall in Imdalind," Mira said, pointing to the map as a whole bunch of blue lines moved from one point to another. "Most of the injuries were superficial, although we did have a few broken bones, and one or two..."

"That doesn't include whiney Magee, right?" Wyn asked, popping some bubble gum as she pointed to the lone purple squiggle that was with the blue ones in the faint grey lines that I instantly recognized as the main hall inside of Imdalind.

"No. Sia Demarco," Mira corrected, although her lips were already pulling up into a smirk, "has been moved to Imdalind. She has received her honorary bite--"

"As it should be," Talon grumbled under his breath from where we stood by the chairs, the muscles in his arms flexing as he crossed them over his chest.

"--and is with the other Chosen in the recovery hall," Mira

continued without turning to the still mumbling Talon. "Her parents seem to be pacified for the moment, but Giovanni is already causing rumblings in the lower meeting hall. They all want to know what punishment our Undermortal faces."

Even Mira reference the girl with enough disdain that I flinched, my unruly worry of the girl mixing with Talons threat of before in an awkward guilt-concoction that was making everything spin. Although that may have been more from my magic trying to connect with my mother's. She stood before the map; her eyes blacked out as she looked into something. I shoved my hands in my pockets, clenching and unclenching my fists as I forced myself to bite my tongue and stay out of the conversation.

Talon didn't have the same will-power.

"She should be locked in the dungeons after what she has done," he snapped loud enough that everyone was forced to turn this time, his muscles still flexing when he tried to burst through the inner ring of powerful Eternals. It only took one stern look from my father to send him to a halt. Although he didn't back down. "They are still down there, I know. They were built for those that break the law--"

"Talon, those dungeons were built in a time of war that spanned over centuries of love, loss, and bloodshed. To have you suggest we use them in such a way is a disgrace to your family and your namesake. I have told you before that we do not rule with discrimination and fear, but with love and compassion," King Ilyan roared with a sound that rattled the stone, the magic in the air pressing against my bones.

No one else flinched. I guess I wasn't the only one that had been stubbornly fighting against my parents the past few weeks, the look in their eyes made it clear they had done this with him before.

I took a tiny step back, however, carefully avoiding the dark stained stone.

"Compassion for who, father?" Talon roared nearly as loud as he took a step forward, trying to stare the man down although he stood a good head below him. "Compassion to the Chosen or to the--"

"All of the people who live in this realm are our people. All of them. Do not make me warn you again, Talon!" I wasn't sure if it was his magic or the level of his voice, but I was pretty sure the rock beneath my feet was shifting.

And I took another step back, even Patrice looked a little shaky at the anger that was dripping from the walls. Considering she had been allowed in the room for decades, I had a feeling this usually wasn't went down in here.

"I don't--" Talon's snap didn't get past two words before he was lifted into the air and turned upside down, his shaggy hair flopping around as he flailed his arms and mumbled and screamed behind closed lips.

"Damn. I just wanted to shut him up before I punched his jaw in." Aunt Wyn said, hands on her hips as she looked up at my still flailing brother. "Didn't mean to Back to Future you, dude. You look like George McFly up there, complete with comb-over."

"That was me," Mira said, standing beside Wyn, both of them with big ol' smiles on their faces. "I figured if he was going to talk out of his ass, that part better be up."

I didn't know whether to laugh or high tail it out of there. I mean, my family was weird, but this was an uncomfortable combination of insanity I had never seen before.

Talon was still strung up by his ankles, mumbling and gesturing as he very clearly tried to curse everyone out. I had seen that look in his eyes enough to know what was on his mind.

Probably something to do with how we are all wankers.

"We all ready to talk civilly?" My mother asked with a bit of a snap. Her eyes had returned to normal, "Or am I going to have to make you hug it out?"

She narrowed her eyes between Talon and my father, verbal reprimand given. And a mental one judging by the tight-lipped stare from my father, who was now moving lines around the map with little thought of anyone else.

"Perfect." She continued once Talon had stopped mumbling and mentally cursing everyone out. She snapped her fingers, sending Talon down into a heap, and both Wyn and Mira giggling as they returned back to the map.

"Would you like to try again, son?" Father asked holding his hand out to a gasping Talon. His face was still red and heaving as he glared at the towering king, but he still took his hand, letting him pull him to his feet where he stood and winced.

Everyone was looking at him, everyone but Patrice who was leaned into Dramin, whispering something I couldn't hear. She wasn't using Czech, which was what my family normally spoke, and before my brain could define the language she had stopped, kissed my brother on the cheek and strode out the door behind us.

No one but Dramin and I noticed. They were all still staring at Talon, waiting for him to 'try again'. He looked like a child being scolded, well a stubborn child with a jutting chin the size of a monster.

It would have been the perfect image, if my dad wasn't oozing so much power the stone beneath my feet was still rattling slightly.

"What are you going to do to it... to her," he amended that last part when Wyn cleared her throat.

"Gemma," my mother corrected, moving the single green line from the yellows that denoted the mortals over to the outline of

Imdalind. "Will be attending school. Mira will be controlling her magic with a tricky little shield that she developed back when she had a little problem in Japan."

"It's a fun one, it's like an on-off switch for tyrants." Mira prattled with her usual grim expression when she was playing guard. "Although I might add the whole," she turned to Wyn. "What did you call it again?"

"Back to the future." The two were smiling again. I had a feeling my mom would be right by them too with the way the corners of her mouth were turning up. But she was all Queen right now.

"Yeah, that," Mira said, folding her arms over her chest. "I might Back to Future her whenever she's out of line. It'll be fun."

"Don't make me question the decision to put you in charge of Gemma, Mira," Ilyan growled, still staring over the map.

"What do you mean, in charge of her?" I asked, regretting at once when all of the rage that Talon had been holing away turned to face me, his eyes narrowing in the same look from before.

"Mira will be following her day in and day out until we know for sure that she is no longer a threat to her. To anyone, really."

"So, like the Russian Mafia in the 1960s? Because I almost joined then and I would be glad to take up that mantle if needed." Wyn said, an eager glint in her eye. Everyone stared at her before turning back to the conversation.

"We have given her a chance, but she must prove herself worthy of it." My mother was sounding a bit too much like my dad.

"Or she will go to the dungeons?" Talon asked, his jaw tight as he clearly tried to control his temper.

"Or something like that," Mom wasn't even smiling, I had a feeling that answer wasn't anywhere near the truth. "The goal is still to unite our people, and this is an unfortunate backstep.

Right now, we need to keep all parties as happy as we can. Wyn has told me the situation in the tunnels is worse than we feared. If we send food and supplies there, as well as increase the public appearances and goodwill to the Chosen families it should begin healing on both sides and get us back on track."

They all began nodding in agreement, plunging right into discussions about who is going where and why. Well, all but my brothers and I. We were left watching them like weird spectators, scowling spectators in Talon's case.

"Somehow, I always thought Council was cooler than this," I said, sinking into Patrice's unoccupied chair besides Dramin.

"Council is cooler than this," Dramin said, staring at the back of our scowling brother's head. "This was not Council."

"Then what was this?" It was hard to admit the balloon of acceptance that was deflating inside me.

"This was Talon's rage hour," Dramin chuckled as our aunts and uncle left.

"Is that why Patrice left?" I asked with a glance toward the door.

"Believe it or not, you are not the only person who has a hard time dealing with our meddling older brother." Dramin wasn't smiling.

"You mean leaving is an option? Because if I can slip out and not witness--"

"Not for you, Row. You have to stay." Talon whirled around, his face as fiery as it had been when he went toe to toe with dad. "Don't tell me your wife ran off, Dramin. Couldn't handle it? I don't know why you bonded yourself to her."

"Love and Compassion, Tal," Dramin said with a nod of his head. "Someday it'll make an impact on you."

"The only thing I want to make an impact on is--"

"Talon," Father said from right behind him, cutting him off

and causing him to jump a good foot in the air. So much for the big powerful butthead. The guy whimpered.

"Yes father?" He didn't turn, he stared straight ahead, trying to rearrange his features as if he didn't have an audience.

"Come for a walk with me." It was not a question, and our dad was already heading toward the door in expectation.

"Have fun, Tal," Dramin said, both of us wagging our fingers at him in farewell.

Talon audibly growled; whatever profanity he had been about to send our way repelled by one look from the King. Seconds later the chairs we were sitting on vanished, sending us tumbling to the floor, and Talon howling with laughter as the door shut behind him.

"God, is he ever not a douche?" I asked as we slowly picked ourselves back up, Dramin moving me out of the way as the magically reappearing chairs tried to land on our heads.

"I'm still waiting for that magical moment," Dramin sighed. "First to witness it wins a hundred?"

He stuck out his hand and I gladly took it.

"Deal."

We shook once and headed toward the door, Dramin silent and still and wise beside me. Just like always.

"Dramin can I ask you a question?"

"Always." He smiled, though he was still looking at the door, hands plunged into the pockets of his bloodied jeans.

"If you knew someone was good, would you fight for them, even if everyone else disagreed?"

He exhaled, his eyes darting to me before focusing back on the door.

"Rowan, do you know why Talon does not approve of my wife?"

I could only shake my head no, the two had been bonded before I had seen five years. Far too young to have concrete memories besides that the cake was good, and the hair braiding boring.

"Because you didn't turn into a womanizing whore like he did?"

"No," he shook his head, chuckling at the truth in my statement. "It all stems from where she--"

"Rowan," my mother called from the middle of the hall, cutting off what Dramin had been about to say. I froze in place, turning to where she sat in a chair, a mug of black water perched on her knee. "It's later."

A rock lodged itself in my throat, it swelled and burned until I couldn't do much more than sputter and gasp, everything from stomach to throat suddenly tight and uncomfortable.

I knew exactly what later meant, and why she had that mug on her lap.

I hadn't been brought here to witness Talon throwing a hissy fit, or join Council. I was sure she thought this would be more comfortable than the frightening underground cave she had first taken me too.

I still wasn't interested.

"We can talk about that later," Dramin whispered, his hot hand on my shoulder feeling like a bomb. I gave him a brief nod, suddenly struggling to find the power to speak. "Good. See you later, baby brother." Dramin clapped me hard on the back, sending me stumbling forward. "I'll see you at Friday night dinner, Ma!"

She lifted the mug to him in farewell, the slam of the door closing coming only a second later. But I still couldn't move, I was trapped. There was no running away from a powerful, immortal Drak, and after what I had admitted earlier I might as well be locked in a cage with what was about to happen.

"I really don't want to have this conversation, mom." I finally forced out, the words distorted by that damn rock that was now trying to fuse itself in my chest.

"If you are having sight then we need to have this conversation, Rowan."

"I'm not having sight, I'm having drea--"

"Dreams, I know," she cut me off before taking a slow sip from the mug. "I had dreams too. Some good, some bad. Your Uncle Dramin, whom you never got to meet, was the only other Drak I really knew. He taught me that those dreams were sight forcing their way out."

"Or they are just dreams," I said stubbornly, still refusing to move.

"Fine. Then how long have you been dreaming of her?"

There was nothing I could say that wouldn't give me away.

"A while."

"And how long have you known she was the one behind the attacks?" She didn't seem nearly as disappointed as she should be. Especially after seeing my Dad and Talon go at it. She was still looking at me with that same gleam of pride her eyes. Her son, the Drak, who could do no wrong.

The truth of it cut against me like a wire brush, digging into my emotions until they were all raw and unwanted.

"A while," I was grinding my teeth together now. "Mom. I haven't changed my mind. Not from ten years ago. Not from last week. And not from this morning when you left that mug on my desk."

"Different mug," she teased, ignoring my rambling frustration.

"Same poison." I pushed "I'm not going to drink. I don't want to see where all these bloodstains came from. I don't want to see what's burning. I don't want to feel responsible when I can't stop *another* death!"

"No one has died--"

"But they will," I interrupted her, grateful when she didn't go all commanding Queen on me. "And I don't want the blood on my hands when that happens. When I fail to stop it."

"Honey, I think--" Her words cut off as though she had hit a brick wall. Her face going blank as she turned to the main door of the room a second before Ilyan burst back through, Ryland and Mira right behind them.

They all looked terrified.

I had been ready to argue, to put my foot down and make a stand, but seeing the panic and fear that was peeling away from them all took it all away.

"How bad?" Mom asked, the mug left in the middle of the floor as she rushed toward them, my father opening the door wide.

"The roof is gone from what the guard saw." My father began, his voice the same dark rumble of before. "There are a hundred on the ground. It looks like they cleared the Northside Way-home out right before then."

"The Way-home?" I asked, not that anyone paid me any attention. Way-homes were the shelters for Mortals with no place to go. Homeless shelters, my mom had called them once. I had been to one years ago after the first Gauntlet I attended. The place was clean, nice, but full of teens turned out by their Chosen parents after they failed the Gauntlet. Full of mortals who were starving and desperate.

It was shortly after that that my dreams began.

That I began to see how wrong this world is.

But to clear out a way home? To attack a cathedral?

It didn't make sense. Something had happened and I wasn't about to close my eyes and take a peek to find out what. No matter how much my head was spinning.

"We know of at least twenty that have died, although the Skřiteks are battling it, they aren't fighting. And they can't find the original attackers." Mira said as my mother finally reached them, throwing the door wide to escort her through, and let it slam behind them.

"Wait. What happened?" I called after them, seconds before the door shut.

Ryland pushed it open again, he and my mother stood there, my mother's hand wrapped around his bicep as though she had tried to pull him back. My father and Mira had already gone.

"There was an attack, Rowan," Ryland said with as much dread on his face as in his voice. "The Cathedral in Prague is burning; something was written there..."

He pressed his lips together, my mind flashing with a million dreams of Gemma and her people and all their raids. All the times I should have said something.

"But that girl, Gemma..."

"No," Ryland said, shaking her head. "It wasn't her. This time it's the Chosen. They are fighting back."

My mother's magic flared then, a pop pulling both of them out of the cave and into the city where everything was burning. The door slid shut, leaving me alone in the dim room, with the bloodstains that were starting to feel like dark omens of what was to come.

12

SIA

THE AIR DIDN'T SMELL SO MUCH LIKE BLOOD, AND THE WORLD didn't feel so much like pain. In fact, everything felt amazing. It was as though I was made of light, and air, and sparks.

Sparks.

Magic.

My magic.

The last thing I remembered was Thomas pressing the fangs of the Vilỳ into my wrist while Wynifred held me down. Pain was everywhere, growing worse as the poison flooded my veins, awakening my power.

Now, that power was everywhere.

I sat bolt upright in bed, sucking in a breath that felt like my first in years and saw the world with a glimmer that didn't seem real. Like everything was brighter. Cleaner.

Although that could have been because of where we were.

An underground cavern, the ceiling covered with mirrors and metal sculptures that let light shimmer over everything like stars.

"The Caves of Imdalind," I sighed in recognition. I swear I could have felt the buzz of energy in the air.

"You're awake. Shame, I was hoping you would last longer." The low drawl didn't chill me as much as it usually did. Everything was too warm and sparkly for that.

"Hello, Mother," I said as I turned, taking a glance at my wrist and the raised brand in the center. It looked like a fairy, or a dog with wings. I couldn't quite make it out.

I would have to examine it later.

My mother looked as sour as she always did, staring at her phone as she tapped the screen a few times before glancing up at me.

"Your father is on his way," she said. I smiled and she soured further. "This will not be a pleasant reunion, Sia. You nearly failed us."

"Nearly. But not quite. All things considered, I think this is an even better outcome," I said, looking around the massive hall that I had been placed in.

The place was lined with old metal framed beds, each one stripped down to an old blue and white striped mattress. A few were stained, some were ripped, some were missing altogether. But that was it. Me, my mother, and hundreds of forgotten beds.

"Where are we?"

"Imdalind," she snapped, back on her phone already. At least I had gotten that one right.

"Where is everyone?" I tensed, her dark eyes lifting from the phone to bore into me. Although after getting the same look from the Queen I doubt the glance would ever have the same impact again.

The Queen could accomplish it much better.

"Gone, Sia. Gone home, preparing for the first day of Imdalind Academy. You slept through all of it." She wasn't smiling, considering what she had said I would have expected even the tiniest nudge of one.

If I was the last one here, my magic was the most powerful in my year.

"I knew it," I gasped, the old metal bed whining as I twisted, double checking that I really was the last one here. "I was meant for this."

"Meant for what exactly?" My mother snapped, the phone falling down to her lap with a tiny thunk of metal against her starched wool skirt. "Meant to be the last through? Meant to finish behind hundreds of Drains? Meant to fail? Because you did all of that."

"The test was rigged, mother. The tasks, they changed them. They were made for the Drains. Those damn rats all rushed through."

My mother said nothing, she was back to tapping on her phone, her dark eyes darting up to mine when the loud grind of a stone door echoed from somewhere in the distance, the loud echoing taps of expensive leather shoes following right behind. Only one person I knew could walk with such power.

"They cheated, mother. I'm sure of it."

"You think we don't know that?" my mother hissed under her breath as my father stepped into the light. "Everyone has been talking about it. Hardly any of the Golden Children made it through. You, and Tasha, and Miko are three of only a handful. And *you* barely made it."

She looked up from her phone at that last part, her eyes narrowing as my father wrapped his hand around her shoulder. He was staring down at me with as much intensity.

"Father," I nodded my head as I had tried to do with King Ilyan what felt like hours before.

What was it really? Days? Weeks? Months?

"Glad to see you are finally with us. They were considering beginning the school year without you." There wasn't a drop of emotion on his face or in his voice.

You would think after a meeting with the King and Queen

and being honored with their recognition they would be showering me with flowers.

"How long was I out?"

"Nearly three weeks," mother provided, setting her phone down to look at me. To smile at me. Finally. "The longest awakening in nearly thirty years."

"Three weeks? Then why are you...?" I caught myself before the accusation tumbled out. If I had the strongest magic in thirty years, they shouldn't care how I finished. I knew them well enough to know that.

Something else must have happened.

My mother's phone buzzed, a familiar image flashing on the screen.

Gemma. I was sure I snarled with how fast both of them turned to me, eyes narrowed.

"What happened with the girl? That one with illegal magic?" Yes, I was snarling.

The two of them, however, did not answer. They stared at me, vitriol and malice dripping from their eyes.

"Did they recycle her?" It was a polite term we used for when we pulled the Drains out of the sewer and forced them into The Wastelands. The old work camp was close to the radioactive waters, hundreds of unusable Drains lived in old factories and communal camps and were monitored by barcodes implanted in their wrists. A constant reminder of the bite mark that would never be there.

It was the perfect place for her, but I could already tell she wasn't there.

"Where is she?"

"At the Academy."

"What?" My shriek echoed off the far walls of the cave, it bounced in my ears and pricked up my anger into a bubbling wave of heat under my skin.

Magic. God, I was going to love this.

"Shut up and sit back down, Sia," My father growled, his wide hand flat against my shoulder as he forced me down to the bed. I could feel his magic more acutely now, the little sparks of his power reacting against mine. "They don't know you're awake, and we would like to keep it that way at the moment. We need to speak with you before they whisk you away."

"This is a conversation we would rather not have the Eternal scum overhear," My mother continued, tucking me back into bed.

"Eternal Scum?" I shot back up, attempting to keep my voice low, but they pushed me right back down again.

"Yes. They have betrayed us, Sia. They have betrayed all of the Chosen." My mother's tone was a snarling whisper as she leaned closer. "They have brought the vile sub-beings into Imdalind Academy, into our lives, and praised them. Last week they announced their plans to unite us all again, to have the demented mortals live among the Chosen as family. As equals."

Equals.

The word burned through me, muscles tensing as my anger boiled, the sparks of power and magic bubbling right with it.

"'*One culture. One future*,'" my father quoted, his voice twisting around the words as he spat them back out at me.

"They enrolled that girl and her friends even though they did not complete the tasks. Even though they hurt hundreds of our people. Their kind has stolen the magic from hundreds of Goldens. And they let her in."

"She should have been punished. She should have been killed," I cut my mother off, that molten heat that was rolling through my veins picking up a notch, heating straight through to the tips of my fingers to the bed sheet and filling the air with the smell of burning cotton.

My magic was shooting from the tips of my fingers in

dripping energy, like liquid lightning. Just like that girl's, like my parents.

It was beautiful.

"Yes, we think so too," My mother tucked her phone away as she leaned closer, both her and my dad hovering over me. "The Eternals are out of touch with their people. Something needs to change, but not this way."

"What can we do? What can I do?"

"You were enrolled into the Academy on a technicality, Sia." My father began, the bed frame squeaking as he sat on the edge. "You nearly failed us, and if it wasn't for the negotiating skills we have bred into you, you would be home with so many of your friends. Disgraced."

"You nearly are," My mother began, back on her phone again.

"But your power is strong, the strongest in years. You have been raised with the right upbringing, and the right knowledge of the vile, under-bred Drains. You will be going to Imdalind Academy, and you will be helping us from the inside."

I didn't like the way this was building. I would always help my parents, always stand by them. But I had spent my entire life working to become one of the Eternals, and now they were cursing them. No matter the confusion inside of me, however, I had to lock it inside.

"Yes, Father," I said, pushing myself back to sitting as the heavy grind of the door echoed over to us again, this time accompanied by an army of feet. "We need to prove that all that Drains need to die. This bubblegum bitch is the perfect opportunity."

No matter what he thought of the Eternals now, that I agreed with.

"Good," he continued, leaning closer as the footsteps did, his eyes digging into mine. "It will be your job to take her down.

Accidents happen inside of Imdalind Academy after all, and with the prince there, perhaps you can continue with your plan. Bonding to them one thing, but to bring one of the Eternals into our cause," he clicked his tongue, "I believe only you can accomplish that. Besides, the prince is young, he may be the weakest among them, but that only gives you more opportunity."

"Opportunity to what?" I asked in a hush, leaning toward him as Ilyan, Ryland, and Mira came closer, the darkened edges of the room releasing them.

"To use him." He smiled, patted my hand before leaning closer, and wrapping his arms around me.

I stiffened; he never gave hugs. He certainly was putting on an act this time.

"It's the only way to make amends for your near failure, child," he hissed into my ear, holding me closer as my head turned right to my mother, the phone gone now. She nodded in agreement.

I tightened my jaw. He said that like it was a threat. I would gladly kill the Drain, but he sounded like he wanted me to end the Eternals too.

"I am so glad you are okay. We were so worried," My father continued in full voice, his voice cracking in false emotion. He leaned away from me, brushing some of the tangles of brown hair out of my eyes.

"As were we all," Ilyan cut in as he and the others clustered around the foot of my bed. "We were contemplating beginning school without you, but you seem to not want to miss out on the first day."

My father smiled like the dads in television sitcoms did when their children learn some life lesson about magic and friends and not hurting people. The look didn't suit him.

"How are you feeling?"

"Much better, My Lord." I nodded my head, thankful I could do so that time. "All the pain is gone. Everything feels..." I hesitated, actually struggling to find the right word. "Powerful."

It wasn't quite right, but everyone smiled anyway; Ilyan giving a nod to Mira who took two quick steps to me, holding out her hand.

Oh my god. I was going to get to touch her. I could die happy right here.

"That's good to hear. Now, Mira needs to check your injuries as well as your magic, Miss Demarco. The Queen has already healed the power you were given and centered your magic so it is ready for use. But we need to make sure everything is working well."

I nodded again, feigning hesitation as I placed my hand in hers.

Her hands were so soft, so warm, so much better than I had imagined. I almost smiled, well, until her magic flooded through me. The power feeling like hot knives digging into everything. I cringed and tried to pull away, but she held on tighter.

"Don't worry, it only takes a second," she said, sounding as bored as if she was arranging flowers. I was sure she had yawned, meanwhile, I was being stabbed to death internally.

God. Could she get any cooler?

"Everything is in working order," She said, dropping my hand and stepping back to the king. "I can see her strength causing problems for the first little bit, but she seems tough. I got through it. I'm sure she can do just as well."

"Unless she manages to kill a ghost, a maniac and take down an entire government before she turns fifteen, I doubt that's a possibility," Ryland said, peering around Ilyan to give his wife a smirk, one that she promptly returned.

Holy shit. An entire government? She just got cooler.

Right then it was hard to see them as the enemy.

"What do you say, Miss Demarco, are you up for the task?" Ilyan asked, his blue eyes pulling me from his brother.

"Yes," I gasped.

I wasn't sure which task I was agreeing to, however. Both the King and my father were looking at me with equal glares of expectation.

"Good, then we will send you to the Academy tomorrow evening so you may spend the few days before start of term getting settled in. You may spend the rest of your day with your parents inside of Imdalind. I understand this is a rare treat and the Skříteks outside the Hospital will be glad to give you a tour. They will assist you if you have any questions."

"I do have a question," my father cut over whatever Ilyan had been about to say, his voice weirdly subservient. Fitting seeing as his back had begun to curve into a bow. "A question that only my king and his advisors can answer."

Ilyan's jaw tightened, Ryland looking between the king and my father before he spoke, "Well, what is it, Giovanni."

My mother sat still, phone forgotten, looking between me and my father who was now winding his hands one over the other as he exhaled, shuffling his feet in what was unmistakenly nerves.

Nerves.

My father was never nervous.

And I thought I was good at these games. I had clearly been taught by a master.

"As you know, my daughter went through quite the ordeal in an effort to receive her magic," he began with a bit of a stutter, Ilyan sighing in such a way that it was clear he had heard all of this before. "And we are grateful that she was allowed entry. But she has scars, and even knowing that her attacker is at the same school has caused her great anxiety." He paused again, hands still winding as he turned to me, fixing me with a dark look. The threat was clear.

I quickly rearranged my features, forcing out a stuttering breath.

"I don't know... I mean... Is that girl safe?" I wasn't quite sure what I was supposed to be playing into here, so I tried a few statements before my father's eyes brightened, pointing me in the right direction. "I want to feel safe at school, your majesty."

"We want everyone to feel safe in our world, Miss Demarco, it has always been our focus. While I understand that having Gemma present at Imdalind Academy may be causing you distress, we can assure you that measures have been taken to secure everyone's safety and to help Gemma learn to manage her magic responsibly." Ilyan's voice was calm, understanding, and firm enough that the whole thing felt too rehearsed. "Rest assured that if there is any further steps that need to be taken to ensure your safety, we will do it."

Ilyan took one step back, clearly ready to leave the conversation, and the situation behind him. The look he gave my father was one of finality. My father was not one to back down in any situation, but with the king...? He couldn't.

Even I gasped as he stepped toward the powerful Eternal. My heart was in my throat, my magic retreating in fear as the two faced each other head-on.

"There is one thing, my lord," my father said, his voice firmer now. Ilyan stopped his retreat, eyes narrowing. "You could offer her an escort for the first few months of the school year. Help her get her feet. Help her feel safe."

"An escort?" Ryland laughed, before turning to the king and mumbling something in Czech. The language only the Eternals were to know, and one I had been studying since I was small.

If I was going to be an Eternal, I might as well know their language.

"Why do I have a feeling I know what nonsense he is about to throw our way?" Ryland asked his brother, the sounds so low and quick that I wasn't quite sure I had heard him correctly.

"Quiet brother," the king answered, his voice a low rumble. "Hear the man out. Again." Ryland stepped back, Ilyan's gaze still boring into my father as he switched back to the common language. "What are you asking for, Giovanni?"

"It is your son's first year at the school as well. As you are all born with your power, his presence at my daughter's side as her escort would help keep her safe, and help our family as well as the people I represent to feel supported by the royal family in more ways than you have shown in recent days."

Each word was careful, calculated.

"I see what you are saying," Ilyan finally said. His words were as slow as controlled as my fathers; each posturing move was all part of the chess match the two were locked in.

And my father was winning.

My father was taking control.

My father, a powerful Chosen, standing against an Eternal King. And winning.

Perhaps I was wrong to put my faith in the royal family for as long as I did. To not see the power that was already in my blood.

"Well, something to think about." My father was back to his shy manipulation. "I'm sure a day will be enough time to give us an answer? Perhaps she could even wait to leave and join Rowan when he enters the Academy this weekend."

"Indeed." The word was nearly a growl. "Well, if you have nothing else, we will be on our way." Ilyan's eyes were dark as he looked at my father. The man couldn't even restrain the slim-lipped smile that was peeking through.

"No, My Lord."

"Good," he turned to me, his eyes softening. "It was a

pleasure meeting you, Sia. Please speak with the guards if you have any more questions, they will be glad to assist you."

Ilyan spoke very quickly, giving us no room to thank, or bow, or bestow him with flattery before he turned away, the three of them walking back into the dark with straight backs, mumbling in a language that they thought no one but they knew.

Right then I could see what my parents were saying.

They were better than us. Smarter than us. Lords over us.

My blood boiled. My magic steamed.

"What do you say, Miss Demarco," My mother began, adopting the kings exact phrasing from before. "Are you up for the task?"

"I am, but what if the King doesn't agree to Rowan escorting me?"

"He will agree," my father was firm, my mother's laugh following right behind, but neither of them were looking at me anymore, they were staring at each other. A look that was as close to love as they could get passing between them.

"Send the second wave, Samantha," My father said, sending my mother right back to her phone. "Let's show them how bad it can get, and what they stand to lose if they don't work with us."

My mother tapped against the screen, her smile spreading before she looked back up, giving my father the tiniest of nods.

"It is done."

"Then it is your turn, Sia." My father said with a haunting grin that straightened against my spine. "It is your turn to do as we have raised you. Do not fail us again."

"I won't."

They said nothing more before they turned and left, leaving me in the dark.

In their shadow.

13
___

ROWAN

"MOVE FASTER, ROWAN!" RYLAND'S SHOUT ECHOED THROUGH THE sparring room; the underground cave filled with the multicolored smoke that had been his favorite for the past few weeks.

The stuff was thick, easily obscuring walls, barriers, and thanks to the color: magical attacks. Which was why I was on my hands and feet, heaving from the impact of the gut-wrenching assault he had sent my way. At least I hadn't thrown up that time.

"Move faster, move quietly--" Another attack slammed into my side before I could regain my footing, sending me sprawling over the stone floor of the massive training hall as my legs went ridged. "Be silent."

Ryland laughed, his smug face coming into focus as he broke through the smoke directly above me. I grumbled and rolled over, flicking my fingers and sending him flat on his ass. He swore just as loud.

"Be vigilant." I finished the last of the lessons he had drilled into me since I was a toddler.

"At least you remember something," Ryland said, rolling over and pushing himself to sitting, the two of us panting in the swirling smoke. "I was beginning to think I had taught you nothing all these years. Or are you purposefully forgetting everything so you don't stand out on your first day at the academy?"

"Who cares about my first day." Well, besides everyone, because I surely didn't. The look Ryland was giving me said as much.

It had been a little over three weeks from the attack, and the start of term had been rescheduled for this Monday. All of those who had received a bite from the Vilỳ had awakened with their magic, save one. Saturday afternoon I was due to leave to the massive stone institution, which meant I had three days left at home. Three days of pure bliss, not shoved into a monkey suit and pretending to be something I'm not.

Three days.

Which was probably why Uncle Ryland had dragged me here. One last chance to kick my ass until summer break. He wasn't the only one squeezing in last-minute farewells.

This morning it had been a bewitched checker marathon with Angie. Last night, dinner with Dramin and Patrice. I was sure at some point Aunt Wyn was going to show up and drag me to some old ruin where we could blast music for hours while she talked about the way things used to be.

The only person I hadn't seen was Talon, who had 'hooked up' with a few Chosen and booked it to Rome after the Cathedral had been imploded. After our run in after The Gauntlet, and then in the Council hall I was kind of glad he was M.I.A. I had enough on my mind as it was.

"I can think of at least forty newly awakened Chosen who are ecstatic for your first day." Ryland was laughing at me, shoving me playfully to the side.

Something I returned, but with a jolt of magic inside of it.

Okay, maybe more than a jolt. I accidentally sent him skidding across the stone floor and through the fog.

"Not funny," he called, fully aware I was laughing at the dumb look on his face as I sent him spiraling away.

I felt his magic a second before it blazed through the smoke. The bright red attack was heading right for me. Too bad my attacker was also the person who trained me. I exhaled, a shield snapping around me as I vanished from sight. Plastering my back flat against the stone floor, I laid still the attack flying uselessly overhead.

Move faster.

Scuttling around like a crab, I shuffled through the now swirling fog, the dratted stuff giving away my position. He sent another attack my way before I could move more than a few steps.

Move quietly.

Ryland couldn't even follow his own rules. I could hear his shoes tap against the stone. Although, the rubber of his trainers was so quiet that if we hadn't been silent I probably wouldn't have heard anything. He was close, and coming closer. Fanning my hand wide, I shot a ribbon of wind in the direction opposite of where he was headed, the spirals of pastel mist dancing through the air in what I hoped was a false path.

Be silent.

He followed it immediately, rubber squeaking faintly in the opposite direction.

Be vigilant.

Vigilant enough to remember that your Uncle who was trained by a mad king and then spent over two hundred years training an army was not going to fall for that.

I needed to do more.

I pressed my hand against the smoke, shooting a ribbon of yellow meant to incapacitate him into the multicolored swirls. I didn't even wait to see if the attack had hit its mark before I soared to the side, shield snapping back into place.

I wasn't fast enough. Something warm hit against my back, locking through my bones as I landed like a rock, arms unable to catch me. I hadn't even hit the rock floor before the second attack hit. This one from another direction.

"Shit." There were two of them.

"Seriously? You would think I've been teaching you to knit all this time," Ryland called from somewhere through the smoke, a laugh I recognized at once echoing right behind it.

Double shit.

My dad was here.

The back of my neck was prickling, my magic buzzing as it tried to break free from my father's perfectly coiled attack. I needed to move. I needed to be able to fight back, and dad had turned me into a sitting duck.

Ryland always went a little bit easy on me. But my father never did, and Ryland certainly wasn't going to continue his niceties if his big brother was here. The leather soles of the King's shoes grew closer, his magic pressing against the air as he prepared for another attack. Seconds. I had seconds.

Writhing against the stone, my magic finally snapped his bind, sending my arms and legs flailing to freedom. Not even waiting to catch my breath, I shot an attack right at someone's blue eyes and took off into the air, leaving swirls of smoke and two very shocked brothers somewhere behind me.

"Ha! Ha!" I laughed, breaking through the smoke and leaving it twisting behind me like the tail of a kite. One quick round and then I would turn around and pop the two of them off like ducks in a tree. Or wherever people shot ducks. I had no clue, no one had hunted animals for hundreds of years.

Which is probably why I had no idea what I was doing, and why I was shot to the ground without little more than a pop, just like the duck. My father appeared in front of me with a bang and a gasp, the stutter bringing him within inches of my face. His attack was already lined up and ready.

The blast of grey smashed right into my collar bone, sending me back and tumbling through the air as the smoke cleared. A kill shot. It hadn't been full power, but I had felt the ache in my heart. I knew what it was. That attack was meant to stop the muscles, freezing it in place. I was sure both of them had used it hundreds of times before.

"That was a nice attempt, Rowan," Ryland said as his magic caught me, bringing me in for a nice soft landing. "You almost had us."

"You," I corrected, jumping to my feet. The action wobbly thanks to the concentration of magic in my chest as it worked to heal me. "I almost had you. Pretty sure it was just the two of us until a few seconds ago."

I shot my father a look the second he touched down, loose strands of his hair and the long golden ribbon fanning around him like he was some kind of ancient Greek god. I rolled my eyes and the two of them chuckled with sounds so rich and deep that the cave rang like chimes.

"That's the joy of battle, Son," Father said, putting his arm around my shoulders. "Enemies can appear at any time. There is no such thing as a fair fight. You should be prepared for anything."

"I wouldn't call that a joy, at least not one that I need to be prepared for. There isn't--" I caught myself, my neck prickling as the damn Drak powers ignited. I sighed and shook my head, refusing to make eye contact with either of them. I would be fooling myself if I thought they hadn't noticed that.

Considering I was standing before my mother's husband and best friend they already knew what was happening to me. It was like the worst kind of puberty, and I had barely survived that the first time with two older brothers and so many pestering aunts and uncles following me around.

"It is always worth it to be prepared, Son." My dad's arm slid from my shoulders as he came around to face me, both of them staring at me with the bright blue eyes that I had been jealous of for so long that I almost resented them. "The future is a fickle thing, and even what we see can change. No one saw what was coming at The Gauntlet for example."

I had never heard a statement so loaded before, but I kept my focus on him, refusing to let up. If he had something to say, he could say it.

"No one knows what will come after."

I would give him that. I had been dreaming of the girl with the mohawk, Gemma, for years. But since I had come face to face with her everything had stopped. Perhaps because I had been pushing everything away with every drop of strength I had, but it wasn't something I was interested in understanding, or even fixing.

I had seen what was coming, but I hadn't been able to save anyone. I hadn't been able to do anything. Just like before, I wasn't interested in playing with a power that only caused harm.

Not after what Talon had said. Not after what my father had said.

"I can't see the future," I gave my dad a look, making special care to let my words sink in. "And even I can tell you that it is nothing good. I mean, how many times has Giovanni Demarco stormed through the halls this week?"

"Which is why we need to be prepared." Ryland stuck the final lesson home, like a rugby coach after a good inning. Fitting.

I sighed and pinched the bridge of my nose. The smoke had

cleared now, but I would gladly take it back, and wipe out the looks on their faces.

"Are you guys serious? Speeches on vigilance and preparedness?" They gave each other a look, any pestering they had been planning sliding into oblivion. My heart sunk, the uneven beat falling into nothing. Yes, they were serious. "What happened?"

Ilyan gave us both a look before he continued toward the door, gesturing us both after him.

"Sia's awake." He sounded like he was announcing a funeral rather than a birth of a new Chosen, and new magic. Even Ryland was looking uncomfortable.

"I suppose Giovanni will be storming the halls in all his grandeur?" And stinking up the place, too. I didn't know if it was his magic, or his cologne, but there was always a stink that followed him around.

"He's already come and gone." My father's mournful tone was flooding his face now, his eyes downcast as he looked toward the door. Talking to Mom more than likely.

"Leaving a tidal wave of destruction in his wake, no doubt," Ryland chuckled. "Hopefully he won't cause any more issues now that his daughter is awake and humming with baby magic."

The laughter died away, the tone and temper of their voices dropping the closer we got to the exit of the massive practice hall. I tried to fall back a step, sure I was eavesdropping, but they followed suit.

"We got lucky." My father continued, giving both Ryland and I a side glance. "Sia slept longer than anyone in over thirty years."

"Three weeks?" I asked, my mind wracking through all the histories. I know I had heard of many people waking from the bite long after that.

"Yeah." Ryland laughed, running his hands through his hair.

"Remember when me sleeping for five months was 'not long enough'. Or Joclyn's eight-month coma?"

"I'm glad no one has slept that long, lately." My father's voice was still dark, booming right along his footsteps. It was making the whole conversation that much of knot in my gut. "Imagine how much worse things would be if they all slept that long, and had the magic to match."

"I don't even want to think if it," I mumbled under my breath, my mind was suddenly full of that moment, when Gemma took down the Gauntlet.

"Even without the months of sleep that used to be, Sia's magic is still powerful. Which I am sure will create some problems for anyone around her for the next few years." My father was looking at me, I was stubbornly ignoring him.

"Yes, because we've never had problems with the offspring of douchebags who have powerful magic." Ryland rolled his eyes. I had heard enough of the stories of the war to know he was talking about himself.

"We will just need to watch them, all of them." It was as though someone turned a crank. They rotated toward me in tandem, eyes narrowed at what I had said.

"Luckily, it seems that Giovanni Demarco has given us the key to doing just that." He was looking right at me now. The 'proud dad' look I was so used to getting replaced with a tight jaw and furrowed brow that never accompanied anything good.

"Why do I have a feeling that I am not going to like this?"

"The Demarco's have requested that you escort Sia to her first day at Imdalind Academy, and be her liaison for the first few months."

"Escort?" I choked on the word.

"Yes. Be with her, accompany her..."

"I *really* don't like where this is going." It wasn't the first time something like this had been suggested after all, Talon may not have been less heavy-handed. But it wasn't any better this time around. My stomach was threatening to empty itself all over the front of my father's button-up shirt.

"This feels like I am being set-up on a blind date from hell."

"A set-up of the best kind." Ryland was beaming, I scowled at him.

"I'm not going to be forced to waltz around with some Chosen snob--"

"Actually, it's just what we need right now." I stuttered to a stop at my father's interruption, his words frozen and painful in my ears. I had heard him, but his tone didn't match. He sounded like he had eaten something rancid, maybe he had.

I had.

"You need me to date a girl that I don't know, have nothing in common with, and possibly hate?" So much for keeping my voice down. We were back to yelling.

"I've had to do worse," Ryland said softly. "Just stay with her, help us monitor her magic. Help her control it. Be with her as much as you can, Rowan. Until we can calm them down."

"Being forced into a relationship is going to help no one. Giovanni wants this, they won't stop until they get me on an altar, forcing down their lies!" Now I knew where my father's tone from a minute ago had come from, each word tasted foul. Each word was vile, unwanted, shit.

The world had officially gone mad. Everything was spinning, my uncle was looking like someone had smacked him, my father was setting me up with a nut job, and that warm buzzing at the back of my neck had picked up into overdrive.

That was the moldy cherry on top of the foul sundae I was being forced to choke down.

"Rowan. Son. My people had never done such a thing. You know that a match between souls and hearts begins with a match of magic. You can't force that." And we were back to ultrasmooth King. "No matter how much Giovanni attempts to convince us of it otherwise." Well, until that.

"He wants that," I was growling, hand dragging through my hair as I turned from the two madmen that I was really regretting being related to right then. "And you are going to give him that?"

"No, we are going to give him the illusion of that."

My hands fell to my side, my magic running a marathon through my veins even though everything else felt numb. Cold. As dead as Giovanni's grey eyes.

"You can't be serious." I wanted to punch something.

"We need to calm the Chosen after what happened. I am afraid of what they will do if they feel the scales tip too much away from their favor. The additional seats in the Gauntlet had been meant to give everyone a fair shot, to allow more of the Undermortals into our home and begin healing ties between all of our people. She blocked that path." 'She' meant Gemma. *Her*. Although he didn't say her name with nearly as much malice as he did the Demarco's my stomach still dropped.

"Now, every time your mother looks into future all she sees is fire and she can't make heads nor tails of it. You can help us, Rowan."

I had a feeling he wasn't being completely honest there, but I wasn't going to argue it.

"You named me aptly," I said, clenching and unclenching my fists against the worn jeans on my thighs. "You are shoving the entire world on my shoulders."

Ryland chuckled, "Rowan, you have as much dramatic flair as your mother when she was your age."

The mention of my mother was like lighter fluid against my rattled nerves. I had been struggling to control my magic, to control the spinning heat on my neck, but now it was everything. The world was twisting and fading to the dreaded red of sight.

Ryland's jaw dropped to a wide 'O'. Clearly my eyes were fading to black.

I smashed my head into my hands, blocking me from them and them from me, and perhaps even stopping whatever was happening from getting in.

Even I knew it didn't work that way. This was already inside of me, like a disease.

"I don't want to be like her at my age." My hands dropped to reveal a rainbow of pain and frustration on their faces, the two men staring at me in disbelief.

Yeah, I know, I was harsh. But right then I meant it.

Right then I would do anything to scream it from the rooftops. Before I did anything I would regret, however, I turned and walked away.

I needed to get out of this cave, and away from them. If only they would stop following me.

"You know," Father said as they caught up to where I was storming to the large stone exit in the hollow cavern. "When your mother was mastering her sight she wanted nothing to do with it, either."

"What do you mean, either?" I was growling between clenched teeth; she had told me all this before and I wasn't interested in a summary.

"I mean, it was too much responsibility for one eighteen-year-old girl."

"I guess it's good I'm not an eighteen-year-old girl," I said confidently. Tacking on, "Or a Drak," when they both exchanged a look.

"Listen," I said, doing my best to keep my voice level, but everything was brewing too hot under the surface. "I'm going to that damn school. I'll be your poster child, and I'll smooth things over with the Chosen so they don't go blowing up the underground. I'll even date the Demarco girl. But I don't want this. I want nothing to do with this. This," my voice was booming off the walls of the cave now, fingers sparking angrily as I gestured to myself. "This is not safe, and it does nothing but get people killed."

"Rowan, I--"

"No!" I cut my father off, a dangerous move at any time, but this time he didn't seem so much liable to explode as he did disappointed. That was worse, but I plowed on before I lost steam. "I don't want it. Stop bringing it up. Now, I am going to go sleep for an ungodly amount of time because I can't help it, take a shower and prepare to woo your Sia Demarco so her parents don't start a war."

I stomped past them, feet sliding against the stone in my haste to get away. I expected some snide comment from Ryland, a firm reprimand from my father. But there was only silence.

Dripping, awful, silence.

It froze me to the spot, the ice of their frustrations cold against my spine.

"And tell Mom we can have family breakfast Saturday before I leave. I'm sure she will ask." I didn't turn back. I stayed there, hand on the door, stuck somewhere between fuming mad and ultimate regret.

"I love you, Rowan," was all he said.

It almost made it worse, the simplicity. I said nothing as I plunged through the door, pulling it shut behind me, practically racing toward my old KISS albums and my sweat-stained bed. Gross, but anything was better than what I had left.

And what I was being forced into.

14

GEMMA

"Remind me to never trust you again. Ever." Eddy groaned, rolled over, and promptly vomited all over the deep grey carpet of the hotel room they had holed us up in for the past two weeks.

The Skřítek guard that had been placed by the door curled his lip and promptly ran out the door, muttering under his breath,

The air breathed easy at the sudden departure of the towering golden-haired man who had been something like a ghost. A creepy stalker ghost. He had done little more than stare at me, while I stared at Eddy, neither of us talking as we waited for the big ol' doofus to wake up.

Three of the longest weeks of my life. Even then, I think it had something to do with the fact that the Queen stopped by last night with that same weird little creature perched on her shoulder that she had shown up with two weeks earlier.

Rinax.

The thing, with its blue skin and a body of a mutated cat, glittery wings, and face of a man was horrifying. But it was nothing like the tiny creature that bit me. That brown, leathery monster had haunted my nightmares for years. I would never forget the way it screamed as it broke through the pile of trash I had been digging through in my search for food.

Seeing it again in the Gauntlet had brought all of those fears and nightmares back to reality.

Tangles of blackened limbs, long claws snatching and cutting at my skin. Bloodshot eyes wide as its snarling fangs pushed into the skin on my arm. The pain was like fire. Pure agony that I was amazed did not end me.

After watching Eddy writhe on the fancy hotel bed, it's a miracle they hadn't left me to rot in that old tunnel, assuming me for dead. Ed had screamed and moaned for days, until he thankfully fell quiet and slept while I watched weird movies about "marrying a prince" that was playing on every television station.

These people were obsessed.

Last night, however, neither the Queen or the blue Rinax was concerned about the stalker quality of the movies, but rather that Eddy had not woken up yet. After mumbling about needing to speed up the process, the queen had gone all voodoo and put her hands-on Eddy, mumbling in that same weird language, all while the creepy blue dude stared at me.

I half expected another pillar of future water to sprout from either her hands or Ed's chest. But we got nothing. Nothing for hours, until now, the next morning he woke up and vomited all over the carpet.

I think I would have taken the creepy ass predictions over this. This stunk like rotted flesh. Rotten flesh that was now splashing over the front of the nightstand.

"In fact," Eddy continued, wiping a bit of vomit away with the back of his hand. "Remind me to never let you talk me into anything again."

"Surely you don't mean that," I said, throwing a towel at his head. The white squishy thing landed on his shoulder, sliding down towards the vomit as though it was magnetized. He barely caught it.

"Gem. I feel like I ran into one of those old train cars, was trampled by rats who then tried to eat me. Oh! And then I was run over again but this time by a train car that was on fire."

"Sounds to me like your complaining about magic. Are you complaining about magic, Ed?"

"Bitch." He teased and leaned back on the bed, leaving the vomit pile for me to clean up. Gross.

After seeing the queen magic away an explosion I was sure there was some way to clean that up with a snap. But I wasn't about to try. I would probably light the carpet on fire. Which I had already done twice, much to the distaste of our guards.

"This is the worst thing ever," he said so dramatically that I knocked my fist into his shoulder. He didn't even flinch. "How in the world did you survive it?"

I shrugged and put a towel over the vomit, contemplating if I should try to scrub up the much or not. Cleaning it would at least get me out of this conversation.

"I survived it because I am not a whiny baby." I scowled at him, hands on my hips. "Now get your ass out of bed and clean this mess up."

His eyes grew wide, his lips a tight line, as he stared at me whimpering.

I slugged him in the arm. Hard this time.

"Oh my god, Gemma. Why?"

"Baby," I said, smirking and throwing another towel on the vomit pile. That should smother the gross enough that the smell couldn't get through.

Mission accomplished.

"Of course, I'm a baby. I've been awake maybe five minutes. I feel like my veins are on fire, or full of sewer water, or smothered in flaming sewer water. I'm pretty sure I am going to explode."

"Well, explode in this direction. Because it's not my job to clean that up," I said, motioning to the vomit as I collapsed back on my own bed, holey jean shorts and tights stretched over the white bed sheet. Even after a few showers I still felt like a stain against their bleached world.

"Yes ma'am." He gave me a side eye, he clearly wasn't meaning to say that, but the door had opened as a few of the guards had streamed in flanked by a short blonde woman with hair down to her waist, and steel grey eyes. She looked much different when not covered in blood, although her expression still looked like she was ready to eat us.

Figures they would send an Eternal. At least she didn't have that blue thing with her.

"Hello, Mira," I said. Figured since I was on first names with Wynifred she would be included in that. She only gave me a thin-lipped smile, nostrils flaring.

"Gemma," she gave me a nod. "Edward. Nice to see you awake." She nodded to him.

"Thanks," Ed said, his eyes wide as he stared at her. "But, ummm... actually it's just Ed. Gemma calls me Eddy because--" He halted, giving me a side glance as he shifted on the bed, trying to shift himself to sitting again.

Thankfully he didn't throw up this time.

"Because when Ed and I were kids I didn't want him to have a name that rhymed with dead." I gave her a smile and wagged my shoeless feet at her. "And dead sucks."

I could have sworn a few of the guards were smiling. One even restrained a laugh, trying to disguise the thing as a cough.

"Well, Eddy," she emphasized his name this time. "It's nice to see you awake, and just in time too."

"Just in time?" I didn't like the way it sounded. "Is there a Gauntlet part two that we have to run?"

"No, not at all. School is officially starting tomorrow and we would like very much for you both to be there. We have come to do a few checks and transport you to the Academy so that you can join your peers." She was smiling, although her eyes were still that clouded steel color. She didn't look happy about it at all.

"So yes, I was right. Gauntlet part two." I glanced at Eddy, expecting a smile, a head nod, fist bump, something. He was sitting on the bed, staring at his fingers as little sparks of blue shot into the air like drops of water.

I guess he wasn't hurting as much anymore.

"Magic, Gem," he whispered, not looking away. "I have magic."

I don't think I had ever seen Ed smile so big. He sat, his smile squishing his eyes as he focused on the magic, on the way it jumped, trying to make it mutate in some way. Any joke was lost in the amazing wonder that I still saw in the kid's eyes when we brought home food.

"Well, yeah. What did you think was going to happen?"

"How is this possible? It looks so much different than yours." He didn't look away from his fingers.

"You were bitten by Rinax," Mira said, leaving the guards behind as she stepped between the two beds, her focus darting between me and Ed as though she expected us to attack.

"The blue guy, right?" I asked, leaning forward like the children when the elders told them of how things used to be.

"Yes," Mira nodded. "Rinax is the first of the Vilÿ's and the last unpoisoned of the creatures left. Edmund, the mad king, mutated the rest into horrible vile things that were more likely to rip you apart than kiss you. That was what I was bitten by, on the day the war began and Prague was destroyed. It's what you were bitten by,

Gemma. Those bites were different than the bites from the Vilỳ that were captured, and that the Queen was able to partially tame and heal. They give a different power than their mutated selves, and their healthy ancestors. They all awaken different magic. Different strengths, different focuses. The diseased Vilỳ for example no longer give eternal life, and their healed counterparts no longer awaken the full breadth of power. If we had known that the magic would be as weakened and diluted as it is, we might not have tried to heal the creatures at all."

"Diluted?" I leaned even closer; something was hidden there. I wasn't going to miss it.

"Yes. Those bitten by the partially healed and tamed Vilỳ after the Gauntlet do not possess magic as strong as those bitten by the diseased Vilỳ from the war, and they do not possess magic as strong as those bitten by a healthy Vilỳ, such as Rinax. Who was the one to bite the Queen."

"So you are saying I am more powerful than Gemma?" Eddy said, sparking fingers forgotten as he gave me a wide toothy grin.

"And that I am more powerful than the Chosen?" My magic buzzed, stomach twisting with possibilities as if my magic knew what was said, and what it meant.

"Not exactly." Way to throw water on my fire, Mira. "It all depends on how long you sleep. Which is why the Queen was here last night, and why I am here this morning."

She held out her hand then, palm up, as she stared at Ed. We both stared at it as if something was going to happen. She better not have that freaky Drak magic too, or else I was going to take myself straight out of here. Hide in the bathroom or something.

"Give me your hand, Ed," she whispered with a gasp, as though her voice was made of magic.

Eddy gave me a look, like I was going to tackle her down and protect him or something. My three run-ins with Eternals have taught me one thing, however, they always have a way to get what they want. I sat back against the headboard, feet up, arms crossed.

"Go ahead, Ed," I taunted. "I want to see what she does. Can't be any worse than what the Queen did to me."

He gave me a bit of a scowl before he tentatively dropped his hand in hers, a gasp pressing past his lips as she stared at him. I expected sparks, lightbulbs to burst, skin to catch fire. Something. There wasn't a damn thing.

"How disappointing."

"Why is everything so hot? Why are you stabbing me?" Eddy gasped, he was clearly trying to pull his hand back from her, but even with her light touch it was clear that she wasn't letting him go anywhere.

I was on my feet in seconds, even though I was pretty sure what was going on. It had been this painful when the Queen had centered my magic a few weeks ago, although I could have sworn she did that to him last night. Didn't matter. One step out of line and I would throw Mira against the wall, anyway. Deal with the repercussions of that later.

"What's going on?" I snapped, Eddy still struggling against her.

"I'm monitoring your magic. Checking strength, ability. Making sure everything worked right last night when the Queen came to center your magic and pull you awake," Mira answered. Well, I was right on one of those things.

"What the hell does that mean? Pull him awake? I thought you said that everyone slept for different times?"

"Yes, well, your friend Ed here is a special circumstance. You're smart, Gemma, you surely put it together by now that no one knows of Rinax's existence." I had, but I wasn't about to show any more cards than that. I gave her a nod and sunk down to the bed just as she released Ed's hand.

He reeled it back in like it was on a fishing line, frantically rubbing his palm.

"You received a bite from the first Vilỳ, Ed, the last real Vilỳ. That's a lot of magic. We would rather that information not get out. Instead of allowing you to sleep as long as you would otherwise, we pulled you awake so that you can start school with the rest of your peers, and hopefully with the same amount of magic." She smiled. Ed and I exchanged a look.

This whole thing was starting to feel like a trap. And we had walked right into it. Wooed by the chance to continue a revolution. A revolution on puppet strings.

"So, you used some special pumped up thing to bite him? Great. What do you want in return for this great gift?" I spat, jumping up from the bed again. "No one just gives people who tried to blow you up superpowers."

Mira looked like she was about to laugh, "Think of it as a show of good faith on our part."

"That doesn't answer my question, what do you want in return?"

"We want the same things, Gemma, Joclyn has already explained that to you. This is all only to help in that. To help heal our world."

"Nothing is ever that simple." I scoffed. Mira only smiled before she stepped back to her guard, one of them handing her a small pouch. The black velveted bag was so small I probably wouldn't have noticed it if the guy hadn't heaved a sigh of relief on its hand-off. Like Mira had taken a thousand-pound weight from him.

"Well, either way. You'll be happy to know that your magic is in working order, Ed, even with the early awakening." She gave Eddy a tiny grin, "that's only part of why I am here, however."

Mira's smile faded as the guards took one simultaneous step forward. Screw this badass standoff, I took one back too.

Mira spread her palm between us, emptying the bag into her hand. Tiny little pebbles spread over her palm, they looked like little more than dust. Haunted, frightening dust that might have been mined from the souls of the damned. The stuff almost seemed to be glittering. Pretty glitter, that judging by the racing energy that was assaulting my veins, I should be very very scared of.

"I don't know what that is, but I am not interested." I took another step back.

"One of your conditions to keep your magic and attend the academy was to have your magic bound. This is a piece of an omezující stone." She looked at me like I should understand what she was saying. No, like I was supposed to be scared. Well, I had already had that down, and with her tone, the fear was growing.

I screwed my face up, pushing the knot in my stomach away. I refused to be scared of a bit of dust.

"And what are you going to do with the Omjuki, Omzi... with that stuff?" I had run out of room to step back and had now backed myself up against the night stand, which was great because now she was stepping forward closing the gap between us.

"When embedded in your flesh it will restrain your magic enough that you will be able to learn to master it. If you do that, if you prove yourself worthy, then the stones will be removed."

"And how... How do you plan to embed them?" God, that sounded awful. No wonder my voice was stuttering. I took a glance at Eddy, hoping he hadn't caught that. The worry in his eyes promised me otherwise.

"Have you ever heard of a Štít?"

15
———

ROWAN

MY PARENTS LOVED THEIR JOKES. OR RATHER, THEY LOVED torturing me and my siblings with things they thought were funny. Seeing as Talon was over forty years older than me, Dramin only a few decades younger, and my little sister barely eight. I was all they had right now.

Which was probably why I was being forced to ride to the first day at Imdalind Academy in a horse-drawn carriage that I was sure was a relic of my father's childhood, thousands of years before. The thing reeked of dust, mold, and that sweet perfume old ladies use to cover up the smell of dust and mold.

Although that stench might be from the girl who sat across from me.

Sia Demarco.

The girl who had 'faced the terrorist' and been given an 'honorary enrollment for her heroic efforts.'

It was all bullshit, even if she didn't know that I knew that. I had seen enough of her 'heroic actions' in my dream to know I wanted nothing more to do with her than I did with my father's homemade Listy. His favorite leaf stew was foul and always made my stomach spin, just like the scent that was coming off her. She had clearly bathed herself in some perfume meant to ensnare me.

Not that she had to try, I had already been commanded to 'escort' her for the first few months. Although, my first assessment of having been sold off to some girl in a 'royal match' was beginning to feel more accurate. Especially considering that her parents had been on hand to see us off, snapping pictures and demanding I put my arm around her as well, kiss her cheek, hold her hand, and many other atrocities. They got none of them. With a sniff from her mother and an eye roll from mine, they closed us in a carriage that felt like something you would see in a wedding march.

Or a funeral dirge.

I was going to go for the latter. It was going as slow as one, perhaps I could use a bit of magic and prod the horses that dragged us along to go faster.

I sighed and shifted my weight, still trying to dodge her intense stare. She really needed to find somewhere else to look.

"So, Rowan," Sia began, clearing her throat with a sound that I was sure she thought was ladylike. I shifted my weight, but didn't turn, choosing instead to keep staring out of the draped window as if there was anything to look at besides trees. "Are you excited to begin your training at Imdalind Academy? I am sure it's been a long wait to gain your magic like the rest of your family."

She sighed like the love sick crown chaser she was, her eyes glazing over until a tiny laugh cracked from the back of my throat. She narrowed her eyes at me, a bit of her father's scorn shining through.

Oh crap, she was serious.

My magic was part of me. It was naive of her to think otherwise. I wasn't interested in correcting her, however, there were too many other questions that came along with that.

"Yes, I am excited to be there with all of you." My throat burned as the lie slid through it, but it pacified her. She was back to smiling and sighing and leaning against the old springed seats as the carriage bounced along.

"I am so honored to be able to go to the Academy. I wouldn't have made it through the Gauntlet, not after what I ran into."

She was back to sighing dramatically, crossing her legs slowly and allowing the blue, grey, and red plaid of her crisp uniform to pull above her knees. I was going to be sick, and I had weeks and weeks of this to look forward to. I was suddenly wishing I hadn't slept for the last few days. I had five days before I would need sleep again, and would be able to lock myself away from this mess.

It couldn't go fast enough.

"I couldn't walk away from that. So many more people would have gotten hurt if I wasn't able to intervene," she continued after a few minutes when I didn't respond.

Shame. Looks like my attempt to continue this trek in silence was not going to happen.

"Yes, it was an unfortunate circumstance," I said, keeping my voice monotone and my focus out of the carriage. "I am glad it was not worse, so many people could have been killed if you hadn't intervened."

My focus darted over to her when she sighed dramatically again. It was like she had sprung a leak, or had bad gas, no wonder a bright smile was spreading over her face.

Gas or not, I had to admit Sia Demarco was pretty, if only because she hadn't inherited her mother's sour expression. Long chestnut hair hung over her shoulder, a bit of red catching in the light. Her eyes shimmered in a blue-grey that I wasn't sure was natural, but stood out against the few freckles of the bridge of her perfect nose.

She knew how beautiful and desirable she was, and that

confidence only added to the beauty. It was the smug, rotten, lying soul behind the glint in her eyes, however, that was making me wish we could get there. Then I could lock myself in my room and away from all the baby Chosen.

Away from her lies.

"Yes, I was so very lucky to have been there when I was. Luckier to have run into that girl so I could try to stop her. I wish I knew more of what to do. I didn't know there was still illegal magic in the world. I wasn't prepared." She sighed again, leaning forward as she looked at her hands, little sparks jumping between her fingernails.

Luckily, she seemed to control it okay, I didn't need to be extinguishing a burning carriage while frightened horses careened down the street. I put a shield around the carriage anyway, not that she noticed.

"Well, now you will learn about your magic and know what to do in the future. And she will know how to control her magic so that things like this don't happen again." I chose my words carefully, turning back to the window in what I hoped was a conversation ending action. Too bad the sound of a deflating balloon from the other side of the carriage was making a grand return.

So much for the raging beauty. Her lips had pursed, her nostrils flaring as she breathed.

"Is that why the terrorist was allowed to enroll in Imdalind Academy, Rowan?" I guess she had inherited her mother's sour expression after all.

"I don't believe the girl to be a terrorist. A rebel maybe, but nothing more." I was trying to be calm and indifferent; she clearly wasn't taking it that way.

Her eyes flashed darkly as she sighed, leaned forward and whispered so low she must have been concerned the horses would hear seeing as they were the only ones within fifty kilometers of us.

"A rebel? You can't be serious?"

"I am." I looked right at her, letting my magic wash over the air in an angry wave that although she couldn't detect she still flinched. "She was standing up for her people. For their rights. For what she thought was right."

I wanted to add that my parents had done the same thing, that I would do the same thing, but she looked about ready to explode. Instead, I bit my tongue, straightening my suit jacket in a need to keep my hands busy.

"She maimed hundreds of Goldens. Your people." I wanted to tell her that they were all our people, and that none of them were, but that previously controlled magic was starting to smoke. "I saw the blood. I felt that pain."

"The great war between magic was worse," I mumbled going back to the window. They were some of the first images I had been cursed with, nearly ten years ago, back when I thought being a Drak would be fun.

I still heard the screams sometimes.

"If she wanted to kill you, she would have." I spoke in full voice, turning back to her as the carriage hit a pothole and we both went bouncing. "She's been blowing up massive buildings for months, and somehow you came out with a few broken bones--"

"It was a broken spine," she cut me off like the injury was medal worthy. I waved her off.

"You were surrounded by Eternals with powerful healing magic ready to help in case an accident like that happened."

"It wasn't an accident!" Magic flamed behind her eyes, and I knew I shouldn't back off. But her lies, her delusions, I couldn't let them rot between us.

"No one died, Sia. No one walked away with anything more

than a bone still bound by magic to mend. She knew what she was doing, and her message was loud and clear--"

"If I didn't know any better I would say you and your family were on her side." Her lips curled dangerously and I cringed, pressing myself back into my chair.

Damn it.

Some poster child I was, I was already failing on the whole smoothing things over with the Chosen thing.

"We are on the side of our people."

"Then will you be on my side? I'm yours. I'm your people, Rowan." She reached her hand out to me in greed of contact, her overly manicured fingers twisting in a longing that I couldn't give her.

That I didn't want to. Tucking my hands against my sides, I leaned forward, eyes wide as I stared into her.

"I already am." I forced a smile that I had seen Talon give a million times, trying to master that darn sex on a plate voice. She visibly shivered so I must not have been that far off. Either that or I looked like a creep.

There was a reason Talon was born first I think; he was better at this stuff.

"Then act like it, Rowan." She snarled, the acid in her voice seeping past her painted on grin. I nearly pulled away.

"I am. I believe there is good in everyone. Her. Me. You." I put special emphasis on that last bit.

"There is not good in everyone, not everyone can be redeemed." Her smile faded as she leaned back again, arms folded over her chest like she was proud of herself. It made my stomach twist.

"My Aunt Wynifred killed an entire race of people before she defected to our side of the war, thousands of years before either of us were born. My father forgave her and without her help everything would have been lost." I knew at once I had said too much, that bit of our history wasn't exactly public knowledge.

Her face broke into shocked awe, the greasy grin pulling at my magic dangerously.

"Is that why the girl is being enrolled in Imdalind Academy? Because your family believes there to be good in her? That it was an accident?"

"Only time will tell, I suppose," I paused, my head beginning to spin as her eyes grew hard and angry. Being trapped in here with her was a mistake, being trapped in this role, in the world, was a mistake.

Perhaps she would understand if I bolted out of the carriage and flew myself the rest of the way there. Doubt it considering she was still under the half-seeded delusion that I possessed infantile magic as well.

"I'm amazed that your mother's magic didn't show her what had happened. Everyone says that Drak magic is the most powerful of all. I wish I had been able to see it in action."

I froze against the hard-cushioned seat as though I had been carved into them.

"It's not as amazing as you would think," I said under my breath, slinking down in my chair as she prattled on and I got myself under control.

"I swear I could feel her power in the air when I was speaking to her. Like a dark buzzing fly inside my head. Did you ever feel that?" She paused, obviously trying to bait me into conversation again, into giving away more information about my family.

I had slipped once, but like hell if it was going to happen again. First, she bats her eyelashes at me with such intensity she might be able to take off. Now she wants information.

"It's a shame that none of your family inherited the gift,

imagine what you could do with it?" She continued on when I didn't answer. She would have more luck talking to the trees.

"What did you inherit anyway? How does all that work? I've heard rumors about differing strengths and abilities among the Eternals, that must be why you are eager to start school, isn't it? Hone your skills. Find out which magical branch you fit into at the end of the first year with the rest of us? I'm glad to see you are able to attend, so many were so worried that you would be too sickly to join our class."

I broke her rambling off with a laugh, the sound cutting through the carriage as we changed course, the break in trees and road giving us a tiny glimpse of the ancient monastery my father had turned into the school.

Rioseco.

I don't think she saw, she was still looking right at me, batting those damn eyelashes.

I leaned forward, green eyes digging into hers. Her breath caught, eyes widening as she sat back in her chair as though she had been thrown there.

"Is that what everyone has been saying? That I'm sickly?" I laughed again. "What bullshit. I have no interest in this horse and pony show. I would rather step away from the whole thing and live my life in peace."

Starting with a quiet cabin in a forest somewhere far north from here.

Sia smiled as I slipped for the second time, her hair swinging around her face in a sheet as she leaned closer to me, the two of us only inches apart as we pulled to a stop, the echoing voice of my cousin Cail bleeding through the sides of the rickety structure.

"It appears we have one thing in common then." Sia stood as the latch on the carriage lifted, the door to the ancient thing squeaking as someone pulled it forward.

"Which is?" I asked, but she didn't respond, she smiled and stepped closer, the top of the carriage brushing against her hair.

"I believe you are supposed to escort me."

I wanted to do nothing less right then. The way she spoke, the low snarl in her voice, the confidence that dripped from her. I wasn't sure if I was supposed to be scared of her or desire her. I wanted neither.

I stepped forward and gave her my elbow, thankful that I was wearing the awful crested blazer that was the uniform of this place. I didn't want to feel her magic. I didn't want to give her power any reason to try to mingle with mine. She didn't have enough control of her power to know how dangerous that was.

I felt her magic anyway when she weaved her arm through mine, the rumbling strength pulling through the fabric as the out of control ability tried to infect me.

Sia wanted me, I could feel it in her power. See it in the look in her eyes as she turned to me and smiled.

"Well, this feels nice, doesn't it? It's like we are a perfect fit." Damn. I guess there was no hiding her end game.

Or what I had been forced into.

The truth was compressing against me, closing in from all sides in the iron bars of the cage I had been forced into. The walls were solid, I couldn't breathe, but I gave her a smile anyway, forcing my back to straighten as she reached up in an attempt to tuck the longer strands of hair behind my ear.

I dodged and pulled her forward, wishing I could chuck her out of this carriage and be on my way.

The walls were growing tighter, just like her fingers against my arm.

"Presenting, the third son of our king and our queen, Prince Rowan." My cousin had put extra flair into my title and I almost sat back down, but the girl was pulling me forward, right out of the carriage and toward the hundreds of students who had gathered to witness my arrival.

Although, with the way Sia was acting, she clearly thought the display was for her as well.

"They forgot me. I did sleep longer than anyone after my bite. Do you think they told him about that? They must have forgotten," she mumbled, and I would have corrected her, but we were already out of the carriage, facing the students.

Facing her.

I hadn't seen her in person since that first night, but there she was, standing with the other Undermortals, arms folded over her chest, pierced lip snarling, eyes digging right into me from behind the soft curls of what used to be a spiky pink mohawk.

I had waited for that moment, but now my emotions were a twisted mess after what she had done. After what her actions had forced me into, and who was hanging on my arm. After everything that Talon and Sia and my parents had said.

Malice. Resentment. Exhilaration.

"Gemma." The word was more of a gasp, a pained call that sent my heart into a vice. Her lavender eyes widened beneath her pink curls, Sia clutching her heart in shock.

Sia little mattered, however. I couldn't look away from the girl that I had seen so often I could have sworn I knew her. Well, until Sia had grabbed my collar, pulled me down to her and planted her lips right against mine.

Her magic flooded me, mine recoiled, and the crowd screamed and hollered in joy at the showcase.

By the time I was able to get away from her grip, however, the sound didn't matter, only the smug laughter on Gemma's face did.

"See, perfect fit," Sia sighed and snuggled against me. "You know there's nowhere else to be but right here. With me."

I nearly slugged her.

Would have, if my cousin Cail wasn't staring at me. If everyone wasn't looking right at us, right at the prince.

And all the rules, and expectations, and power that came with that. All of the responsibility.

Damn it.

I had officially stepped into hell.

16

———

GEMMA

ALL OF MY LIFE HAD BEEN SPENT IN HIDING, AND NOW THESE DAMN royals thought they could tame me by locking me behind enchanted walls. Watching their damn prince lock lips with the bitch who had tried to kill Aria was all I needed to see to know how much of a farce this was.

The whole thing was a damn joke.

"What's so funny?" Eddy asked in a whisper, leaning over to hiss in my ear as I laughed at what was easily the most awkward kiss in history.

"Everything, Ed, everything is just *so freaking funny*," I sighed, turning away from the display and back towards the room they had assigned me after they had shuffled us here last night.

Even more Eternals had escorted us than the last time. Probably because both Eddy and I had some kind of super magic.

Well, he did. I swear I could still feel a dead weight of whatever weird magical mass Mira had put in my chest. I still wasn't sure what she had done there but it made me feel trapped, but with a cage that was inside of me.

'*Your new home,*' they had said upon dropping us off. Funny, we all knew it was a prison.

I raced around a corner and away from the hollers and excitement over two idiots swapping diseases and tried to remember the way back to the line of cells they were calling a dorm.

From the outside, this place looked like the stone castles I had always imagined the Eternals to live in when I was a child. Inside, this place was more of a maze then the sewers back home. Steps went to locked doors, hallways were blocked off, and at least one hall went around in a circle.

At least that was what I had discovered in my attempt to escape last night. Well, not escape so much as find every single crack in this place's security and make my plan of escape.

So, close to the same thing.

"Does this *everything* have something to do with the fact that they have locked you inside a castle with a prince?" Eddy hissed as he ran up beside me, checking around the corner and down the hall for Goldens or the CCC or who knows what.

"Yes," I smiled back at him, following him around the corner to a hall lined with doors, this looked familiar. "Well, that and they are planning on teaching me how to use my magic so I can fight and kill him, so, you know."

"Is he your new target then?" He was serious. His exhilaration twisted through my already tight muscles.

"More like a stepping stone," I turned to Eddy, the guy was still beaming with his signature smile.

Although he looked nothing like he usually did. His ripped Hawaiian shirts and stained cut-offs were gone. Replaced with weird beige pants and a blue blazer that barely buttoned round his middle. Even with the gauged piercings in his ears, and the tattoo of a spider that was peeking around the collar of his shirt he looked like the rest of them.

I may have been forced to flatten the height in my mohawk down to loose curls, but at least I had the dignity to "lose" my skirt, cut down my jeans to shorts, and refuse to give up my sewer stained army boots. There was no question who I was.

"The target has always been to bring down the Eternals from the inside, Ed. We have gotten this far, it's clearly fate that he is here with us."

"Forget fate. Maybe it's prophecy," Ed chuckled at his own joke.

"We'd have to ask their freaky ass Queen about that," I said. He laughed, I didn't. "You wouldn't be laughing if you had seen her eyes go black in that interrogation room."

Or saw your supposed future play out for you in the palm of her hand. But I kept that part to myself. Knowing that the witch could actually see into the future was freaky, but it was also putting a damper on this whole plan. How do you stay one step ahead of someone who can see the future anyway?

Hopefully, it won't be too bad, she hadn't seen me explode that room after all.

"I'm still going to put my money on it being a prophecy."

We turned into another hall full of identical doors. Judging by the numbers above each entryway, we were getting close.

"Prophecies are for children and weak people who need to be prodded to become strong. I don't need help to be strong. I chose that. I am that. Go tell your soft-souled prince kisser about your damn prophecy. Maybe she won't need to push kids off ledges to feel good about herself."

"No thank you, she would probably push me off a ledge just for looking at her," Eddy shook his head, held up his hands and backed away like I was the one about to hurl him off ledges.

"Be glad there aren't ledges here, Ed. Or I'd be dangling you by your toes and watching you piss yourself." I gave him a smile and turned toward the door labeled "Gemma's Prison."

Just kidding, it was labeled five-oh-four but that was essentially the same thing.

"Not anymore. Don't forget I have magic now, too." Gah! The guy was oozing with pride. As much as we hated the world we were raised in, you have to admit that having magic was pretty damn cool.

"Baby magic, Ed."

"Baby, super powerful magic," he whispered, leaning into me.

"Doesn't matter, I can take it. Get ready for some ledge dangling."

"Sorry, Gem, no ledges. Plenty of windows though." He was already eyeing the one at the end of the hall as though it was lined with his death certificate.

"No go, I tried those last night."

"Of course you did," Eddy folded his arms over his waist and leaned against my door, fixing me with the know-it-all look he always gave me when I was being a pain in his side. "Bet you tried every door, walked every hall, and even launched yourself off the bell tower?"

"Naw, I saved that last one for you."

Eddy laughed, I laughed, and so did the girl who tore her way around the corner, an entourage of those damn Golden butt-kissers right behind her.

"Throwing a nasty Drain off of the bell tower," She sneered, "sounds like a great initiation activity. The higher they bounce, the higher the points. I call tubby behind you there."

Eddy only laughed, causing the girl to flinch over what she thought was a great insult. She seriously didn't know us very well if she thought those petty clap backs were going to do anything but leave her with welts.

"Why waste my skills, pretty girl?" Eddy said. "I could make you bounce in other ways, well if I was into your type. I don't usually go for the bitches."

Speaking of welts. She had officially been slapped, and she didn't even realize Ed meant girls, although she was still a bitch.

"Ugh! Like I would... You can't talk... How dare you?"

"I guess the royal brat sucked her brains right out with that kiss, Ed." It was true, and some of the Golden snobs in the back tittered until she gave them a look, silencing them and returning them all to sheep with hinges on their necks.

"Jealousy doesn't look good on you, Gemma." Damn, could her lip sneer anymore?

"Really? Jealousy. You think I am jealous?" I laughed and took a step away from my door, closer to her.

There was no way in hell I was going to let her see where my room was. I had lived with shallow bitches like her my whole life. Giving her easier access to some petty scheme was not on my day one in Academy Hell list of activities.

I would have to deal with her the way I dealt with all the others.

"Honey, you live in your golden palace with your shimmering lies, and you think you know the world." I took a step closer to her, all of her cronies stepping back as I lifted my hand. Her feet shuffled, but she didn't step back, the hatred in her eyes didn't fade. That's fine. I had my own to match.

"I do know---"

"Do you? Because it didn't take much for me to knock you off your tower inside the Gauntlet, and it won't take much for me to do it again." I snapped my fingers, willing the magic I had used a million times before to come to life. But instead of bringing the whirlwind of magic and lightning that I had planned... nothing happened.

No spark.

No flash of light and a bomb blowing up in her face.

I stood; the thunder of magic that was running a marathon in my veins trapped inside.

Rat fuckers be damned. So that's what they meant by restrained. Whatever Mira had put inside of me with that Štít thing had turned my magic off.

"No," I gasped as I looked up, right to her smug smiling face as a flash of yellow that slammed against my chest and sent me back a few feet.

Everything hurt, my knees buckling as I fell to the ground, trying to suck in air from the lungs that didn't seem to be working.

"Shame. Looks like all that drippy illegal magic is broken." She and her minions laughed, the cackling noises echoing in my head as Eddy tried to help me to my feet, mumbling something about getting out of here.

I pushed him away.

I could still feel my magic; I could still feel the buzzing energy.

It was possible to fight this. It had to be.

"You're not knocking anyone anywhere. Unless it's you sending yourself back to the sewers," she said, her eyes boring into mine as I slowly lifted myself to stand, every bone aching with the motion. "You're already on the fast track to that."

She smiled with a grin as long and slimy as her ego, her ugly ass shoes knocking against my boots as I stepped closer.

"I give you a month." She said, her fingers sparking again as she prepared to attack.

This time I moved first, punching her hard in the face and sending her to the ground.

"What in the name of Imdalind is going on here?" Someone shrieked from the other side of the hall as one bolt of magic sparked against my palm.

Newcomer be damned, I sent it right into her smug smiling face.

The attack froze in the air, falling to the floor like Eddy's vomit.

Shit. I had no idea how many of their dumb rules I had broken, but it had to be more than two.

My magic sucked back into me like a rat in its hole, Sia gasping as she stood, blood dripping from her nose.

God, it would have been an amazing image, but the furious scowl of the woman who was staring at me made the flow of her blood turn to the drum beats to my death.

It was going to be really hard to carry out my plan if I was expelled, and she was clearly a teacher, ready to do just that.

"Thank you so much, Professor Analine," Sia said, her voice shaking in fear as she rushed to her friends, all of them fussing over her still dripping blood. "She cornered me and used her magic... I... I didn't know what to do."

Great. So, this is how it was going to be. The bitch was sobbing now, and I had a feeling it had nothing to do with her nose.

"Oh, please," I groaned, folding my arms over my chest and tapping the heavy toe of my work boots against the tile floor. "You weren't singing the same song ten seconds ago--"

"Because I was scared for my life!" She shrieked before I could continue, causing this Analine woman's face to blanche. "I think she still wants to kill me."

"Aw, fucking hell..."

"Language, Miss---" Professor Analine stopped mid-sentence, her eyebrow lifting as she waited for me to finish for her.

Like hell if that was going to happen, even if I could.

"She's a Drain, Professor. They don't have last names," Sia continued to sob, not even bothering to correct the slur that everyone else had been actively avoiding. Analine didn't move to correct her either.

So, I can't swear, but bitchy mc-bitch here can call me *that*.

"Very well, as term has not yet begun, and the rules have not been explained, I will not be handing out punishments for either of you. But watch yourself, Miss..." She paused, smiling right at me, emphasizing the fact that I didn't belong to some family or title. "I would hate for your stay with us to be unceremoniously cut short."

I had a feeling that wasn't going to happen, but I had no interest in fighting either of these two over it.

Another punch, however...

"Is that clear?"

"Sure... ma'am," I added that last part on when her eyes narrowed like she was going to shoot lasers at me.

Bet she could. I wondered if they would teach us that.

"Wonderful," the professor said with a grin, "We will turn you into one of us yet."

I nearly snorted. Eddy, however, was forced to swallow a laugh and instead sounded like he was choking on a rat bone. Both Professor Analine, Sia, and her cronies looked at us like we had lost it.

"Well, thank you for all your help, Professor. Now, if you'll excuse us, I would like some time to breathe after that ordeal," Sia said, nodding once to the Professor before slipping into her room, all four of her shadows following behind.

Which would have been fine, except that the room she had escaped into happened to be the one right next to mine.

So much for keeping the meddling medusa out of my life.

"What is this? Some kind of joke?" I shrieked, loud enough that I was sure they could hear before I dodged my way inside, pulling Eddy in after me. I had no clue if guys were allowed in girls dorms, but who the fuck cared anymore.

They had roomed me next door to the devil incarnate. All bets were off.

"I swear if one thing of mine is out of place, she's going to feel it in the morning." I snarled, going right to the mess of papers they had given me yesterday, the ones I had thrown on the desk with the full intent of forgetting about their existence.

"You can't help but think that this was on purpose. What was it that the Queen said to you again?" Eddy said, sinking down into the overstuffed chair and putting his feet up on the little table right in front of it. I still had no idea what the little thing was for, it was far too low for anything practical.

"You mean that I am in prison and have to help them stop the anarchy that they created?" I still wasn't sure what that meant, the woman was a mystery.

"No, that other thing you told me about, the whole thing about enemies with different skills and allies where you least expect it..." He waved his hand in the air, expecting me to continue, but I was frozen, the paper I had been searching for in my hand.

You better believe I was scowling at it.

Period One: History of Imdalind with Professor Analine Krul

Period Two: Wind-Based Powers and Control with Professor Lexia Stone

Lunch

Period Three: Basic Skills and Harnessing of Power with Professor Georgio Gregario

Period Four: Healing and Defense with Professor Etma Diarius

Period Five (M, W, F): Remedials with Professor Analine Krul

"Fucking hell," I snarled, letting the paper drop to the floor like a dead leaf. A dead, grey, decaying leaf.

"What is it?" Eddy asked, it didn't escape my notice that he was chuckling.

"I have two classes with that woman, and get this. It's Analine Krul. Wynifred's daughter."

"The badass from Last Pyre created that?"

"She wasn't a badass, Ed. And her daughters a bitch." Screw chuckling, he was full on laughing now. "This isn't funny."

"Sure, it is." He said, kicking off his shoes and spreading his toes through the holes in his socks. "We may have been the only two from our group to get through that masochistic shit show, but here we are. Not only do we both have supercharged magic, but we have the son, the nephew, and a niece of the King and Queen right here. You want to make a point? We are in the right place to do it."

"We are in the right place to end everything."

I had said from the beginning that the queen was a fool to bring me here, turns out I was right. Maybe I could see the future better than she could.

17

ADRIAN

"A RIA!" M Y SHOUT ECHOED OVER THE STONE, RATTLING THE LOOSE bits of rubble and the flimsy metal scaffolding that we were using to hold the tunnel open.

The rock shifted underneath the reverberation and I jerked, tensing for another collapse, but it didn't come. One more cave in from this excavation and I didn't think I could convince Last Pyre to continue with the project that had become known as "Adrian's Death Trap". Not that it would stop me. It had been almost two weeks. We had to be close. I wouldn't give up until I found it.

Until I knew the truth.

"Aria," I grumbled under my breath that time, carefully placing the rock from the wall of loose stone on the ground and made my way back through the tunnel to the sleeping rooms where everyone was clustered.

The long tunnel was devoid of people. Rocks and scaffolding piled and pressing against fragile tiles and stone of an old subway track that had collapsed a little over nine years ago. Just weeks after Gemma had been bitten when her and her parents had been in this very cave in search of food.

It wasn't a coincidence this tunnel had collapsed. I had pieced that much together even if the elders wouldn't tell me more than a few hidden secrets.

"Aria!" I yelled the second I burst through the door that concealed the caved-in portion of the subway and raced into the massive hall.

No one turned. They were all clustered around the far end of the huge space, and what looked like ten people who were bringing in piles and piles of boxes. Boxes that were clean and unstained, just like the people that were carrying them. The tall, blonde, ethereal looking people.

Skříteks.

My blood boiled when I saw who was in the middle of the group. Who was smiling and shaking hands and handing out blankets and apples.

That same damn Eternal that Gemma had led down here. The one that had attacked me. Gemma had led her right to us. Gemma had brought war to our door and then left us defenseless.

She had put me in charge and I sure as shit wasn't about to let this happen.

"What the hell?" I nearly screamed, candle ears rattling overhead as I stormed toward the group, all of their eyes turning toward me in varying degrees of shock, fear, and joy. The light in their eyes only made my blood boil more.

"Oh!" Wynifred said, smiling as though we were great friends as I plowed my way over to her. "Nice to see you again!"

She extended one of the fluffy blankets towards me, the grey thing clearly soft, and warm, and thoroughly unwanted. I batted it away, wishing I could do the same to all the others. To pile them up and burn them and remove this damn bastard from our home.

But she was an Eternal, a powerful tyrant that had dislocated my shoulder and destroyed part of our home with little thought. I needed to play this carefully, even if the rippling muscles in my back were ready to take this the other way.

"What are you doing here?" I asked, heart pressing against my throat as I snarled.

"I'm bringing blankets, and food, and a dance-off, as promised." She was still happy, still smiling and still passing out the fluffy things. I batted the one on her hand away with a growl, throwing it into the corner where condensation and rot had a tendency to form.

"Don't take those," I hissed to one of the kids as I grabbed another blanket from them, throwing it back in the Eternals face. "She's probably smothered it in diseases meant to take us all out."

The woman's' smile faded at that, her already dark eyes narrowing at me as she took a step closer, her short stature not even bringing us eye to eye. She looked like a kid.

As useless as I was against her magic, it wouldn't take much to land a punch on her jaw. My fingers clenched together, broken nails digging into my calloused palms.

"I have no interest in taking you out." It was clear she was trying to be calm, but even I could see the tick in her jaw, feel the heat that was rippling off her skin.

"Same with the food," I said, ignoring her. "They want to kill us all. Why would they bring us blankets and food if not to kill us?"

"Because we want you to warm and not starving," Wynifred said, one eyebrow lifting as she gave me a half smile. "I mean, I get that you don't trust us, but it's food and blankets not witches brew and devils' dogs. Not everything is cursed with some spell."

Her smile spread as she took the blanket I had shoved at her and handed it back to the kid, "Go be warm and not starving, kid. Let me deal with your boss."

Evan wasn't even ten yet, his parents had been swept away in a raid years before, and he was at the mercy of our community. He just stood looking between me and the Eternal in clear confusion. Follow his leader or be warm. Because he couldn't have both, because I couldn't give both.

At least right now.

I could if my plan worked. If we found what I was looking for in the cave I could. I needed to get this bitch out of here so I could get back to work. In the end, the kid bolted off, he and a few of the other orphans grabbing more blankets and apples as they took off to their corner.

"Don't worry, I'm not going to poison them," Wynifred said, taking a bite of an apple before turning back to the pile of blankets and some weird padded rolls that looks too plastic to be food.

"We don't want you here," I snarled, fists still clenched as I tried to ignore my need to send her flailing with a well-placed punch. "We don't want this, and we don't need your help."

"You sure about that?" She was now handing out those weird rolls to my people. No one second-guessed the gifts before they took off. "Because I am pretty sure starving, cold people need my help. Seeing as your girl, Gem, started her first day of school today you don't have anyone to knock over grocery stores for you. So here I am, with food, warmth, and good music if you guys will stop playing with the cables long enough that I can set it up. Be a good ruler, dude. Support your people."

She smiled with a grin that crawled up my spine before turning back to the Undermortals that were beginning to clamor around her.

"Listen to yourself, you hypocritical bastard. You can't kill my people then come in here claiming to save us," I snarled, grabbing one of the apples from the crate to my left and hurling it at her. It smacked her right in the back of the head, sending bits of apple over her hair, over the faces of the few Undermortals who had been ready to greedily take her handouts.

She froze, the apple speckled faces of my people blanching as they looked at me, at my anger, at hers. They scuttled away as fast as if the CCC was rampaging our way.

"Nice one. Real adult." She spoke slowly, the temperature of my anger rising as the heat in the air did, as it rippled off her in waves. "Listen, I'm here. I'm helping. Be a leader, a non-hypocritical leader, and protect your people instead of leaving them to die."

"I am protecting them, from you," I yelled the words before I rushed her, ready to face whatever attack came my way, whatever repercussions.

Every head turned at my shout, Undermortals and the Skříteks staring as I swung, my fist inches from colliding with her face when instead of a blast, instead of some attack or act of martyrdom I was frozen in place.

"I can see why you lead," she said with a smile, the faint lines of a tattoo crinkling around her eyes, her mouth, down the arm that she was holding towards me, the fingers flexing as though she was going to choke me. "When all you know to do is fight, you pick the fighter to follow. But leading isn't about fighting and fighting isn't all there is. Go cool down, kid."

Wynifred winked as she snapped her fingers, a wind pooling around me and sending me hurtling through the air like the last time. But instead of a hard impact with the stone wall, I was sent back, through the door I had come in through, and passed the red ex that marked the passage as dangerous. The wind picked up as I moved through the tunnels, passed the stone and the scaffolding and into the pile of stone I had left at the very end.

Rock rumbled behind me, groaning in warning. Before I could move away, before I could run from the danger and take off down the cave, it all began to shift, boulders and rocks the size of the old toilets showering over me, covering me.

Curling up into a ball, I protected myself the best I could shielding head and my already damaged shoulder from the paralyzing rain. In minutes it was over, the rumble silencing into the few rolling stones as dust and stone settled around me.

I wasn't crushed, I could breathe, I could see. I was sure the bitch did it on purpose. To leave me with some kind of shame. Instead, all I had was rage.

Moving slowly, I listened to the stone and what was left of the old metal scaffolding for signs of further collapse. I straightened, rubble falling from me like oil-slick rain as I assessed how trapped I was. What the damage was.

The tunnel hadn't collapsed.

The pile of stone that we had spent the last few days trying to dig through however, had. Rock had broken away, piling up like stairs into a massive cavern even bigger than the one I had been thrown from. Tall brick walls stretched up to several manholes that let in strings of glittering light. The multicolored shafts illuminated old tile images and smears of ancient art similar to those back n Last Pyre. Through it all, rivers of water ran over the old train tracks, the surface rippling and appearing blue in the tiny bits of light.

Clean water. Light.

It was like a paradise, a sanctuary that could hide us all. Save us all, if only for the thing that set in the middle of the place.

An old, rusty cage like the ones we used for the chickens sat in a beam of light. The golden, glittering light highlighting the metal, and the squawking creature inside of it. But this wasn't a chicken. It was a beast with leathery brown wings, and gnashing teeth and a scream that cut against my spine in both fear and unrequited victory.

"I knew it."

TO BE CONTINUED
Continue the story now with ROGUE ROYALTY.

ALSO BY REBECCA ETHINGTON

For the always up to date list of super awesome books I've written, visit here:

www.rebeccaethington.com/complete-works/

THE WORLD OF IMDALIND

The Imdalind Series (complete)

Kiss of Fire, Imdalind #1

Eyes of Ember, Imdalind #2

Scorched Treachery, Imdalind #3

Soul of Flame, Imdalind #4

Burnt Devotion, Imdalind #5

Brand of Betrayal, Imdalind #6

Dawn of Ash, Imdalind #7

Crown of Cinders, Imdalind #8

Spark of Vengeance, Imdalind #9

Flare of Villainy, Imdalind #10

Imdalind Academy

The Gauntlet, Book One

Rogue Royalty, Book Two

Broken Renegade, Book Three (Oct 2021)

Reluctant Seer, Book Four (Jan 2022)

Imdalind Ruby Collection

DEMON LOST, SEMESTER FIVE

MISFIT SHIFTERS (RH)(COMPLETE)
ZERO FOX TO GIVE, BOOK ONE
FOR FOX SAKE, BOOK TWO
FOX CHANCE IN HELL, BOOK THREE

THE WORLD OF THE OKIVAN

OF RIVER AND RAYNN

CATALYST

REQUISITE

SYPHER

THE OTHER WORLDS

THE THROUGH GLASS SERIES (COMPLETE)
BOOK ONE: THE DARK

BOOK TWO: THE BLUE

BOOK THREE: THE ROSE

BOOK FOUR: THE CUT

BOOK FIVE: THE LIGHT

THE THROUGH GLASS BOX SET

ABOUT THE AUTHOR

Rebecca Ethington is an internationally bestselling author with over a million books sold. Her breakout debut, The Imdalind Series, has been featured on bestseller lists since its debut in 2012.

Born and raised under the lights of a stage, Rebecca has written stories by the ghost light, told them in whispers in dark corridors, and never stopped creating within the pages of a notebook.

Find me online
www.rebeccaethington.com
contact@rebeccaethington.com

THE COMPLETE IMDALIND SERIES

BOOK ONE: *Kiss of Fire*
BOOK TWO: *Eyes of Ember*
BOOK THREE: *Scorched Treachery*
BOOK FOUR: *Soul of Flame*
BOOK FIVE: *Burnt Devotion*
BOOK SIX: *Brand of Betrayal*
BOOK SEVEN: *Dawn of Ash*
BOOK EIGHT: *Crown of Cinders*
BOOK NINE: *Spark of Vengeance*
BOOK TEN: *Flare of Villainy*

THE ACADEMY BOOKS
The Gauntlet
Rogue Royalty
Broken Renegade
Reluctant Seer

Find me online in my Facebook street team! We have monthly giveaways, sneak peeks, competitions and more!

Introducing The Imdalind Ruby Collection

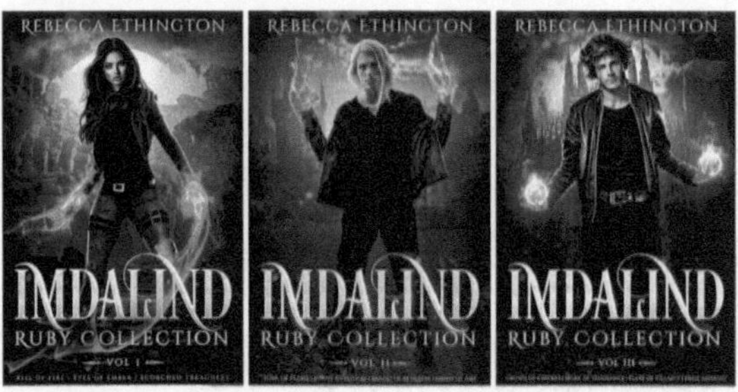

The entire Imdalind Series, in chronological order, with over 100k in new content and point of views. Extended Editions aren't just for Hobbits. <3

Grab your copies now.